Rule 14

I0631000

A Chilling Exploration of the Fight-or-Flight Response

by

William Blackwell

Rule 14

Cover designed by Telemachus Press LLC
Published by Telemachus Press LLC
Paperback ISBN: 978-1-0697318-3-8
Version: 2016.12.22

Acknowledgements

Heartfelt thanks to my loyal and supportive readers, friends and family, the hardworking staff at Telemachus Press, and my editor. Special thanks to the Government of Prince Edward Island for its financial support.

The year had been a year of terror, and of feeling more intense than terror for which there is no name upon the earth.
-Edgar Allan Poe, *Shadow—a Parable*

Rule 14

Prologue

"I didn't want to go all the way," the woman said as the man's hand slid inside her bra and cupped a curvaceous breast. But a seductive smile on her twenty-two-year-old face told a different story. She was breathing heavily, her cheeks beginning to flush red.

She wanted him.

"Come on," the man said, continuing to let his hands roam, kissing her tenderly and full on the lips. "We've been together a long time. I'm so horny."

She moaned softly as a hand gently squeezed her nipple and then fumbled with her bra clasp. He was going by touch, the black curtain of night making visibility difficult.

A grey-blue ray of light from the half-moon outside and the stars twinkling like diamonds cast a suffused glow on her soft features as he continued to work on the bra strap, hoping to free the objects of his desire from their captivity. He wasn't making much headway.

"Let me help you," she finally said. They were sitting in the back seat of a maroon-blue 1972 Buick Skylark parked just off the two-lane highway on a country road near Brantford, Ontario, Canada. There was a clicking sound as she undid the clasp, permitting his warm hands to roam unobstructed over her breasts. He inched closer, rapidly undoing the remainder of the buttons of her white blouse, letting his fingers do the walking.

She moaned softly again, lifted his head up by the chin, and kissed him.

Meanwhile, thirty feet behind them, a man slowly pulled his grey half-ton pick-up onto the shoulder and parked. A grimace contorted his not-so-handsome features.

In the throes of passion, the couple making love in the car did not hear or see him coming.

He extracted his nine millimeter semi-automatic Glock from the crotch of his jeans and clicked the safety off as his brown eyes slowly adjusted to the pale moonlight. His eyes were wild and far away.

He stealthily approached the Skylark from behind, adjusting his black Molson Canadian baseball cap down as he moved. The road was isolated and quiet, but for the odd bird chirping in the night.

The sound of metal tapping on glass—click, click, click—startled the woman and she screamed, jerking away and looking through the window. In the obscurity of darkness, she could see nothing.

She frantically buttoned her blouse as the white lace bra slid off the seat and onto the floor. The man's hands trembled as he pulled up his jeans and zipped the fly.

A booming baritone voice from outside: "Do you have any idea where the fuck you are, lover boy?"

As Lover Boy scrambled to the front seat, the passenger door opened and a bright white flashlight beam shone into his eyes, blinding him.

From the backseat, the woman screamed again.

But for a circular white light and a black silhouette, they could not see the antagonist.

"Shut your fucking bitch up or I'll put a bullet in her head," the man said, flashing the gun in front of the flashlight so they knew he meant business. He knew they couldn't see him or the weapon.

"Honey, quiet please," Lover Boy said, his voice giddy, verging on panic.

The scream echoed into the night and became a soft whimper, like an abused dog cowering from a life of torment.

"Did you hear me?" the armed man said, alternating the beam between both petrified faces.

"You asked me to shut my bitch up," Lover Boy said, fidgeting with his belt buckle. The woman had put her hand to her face to muffle a soft whimper. She didn't want to piss off a man pointing a gun at her.

"Before that, you dumbass!"

"No."

"I said, do you have any idea where the fuck you are?"

"We're about thirty minutes outside of Brantford."

"I know that, birdbrain. But do you know what road you're on?"

"No."

"Well, I'll tell you numb-nuts. You're on Rural Route 14, and it's my fucking road."

"I didn't know it was a private road. We'll leave," Lover Boy said, wiping his nose with an unsteady hand.

The armed man started waving the flashlight around. He still had the firearm trained on the lovebirds. "This is a private road if I say it's a private road." His voice had become aggressive, ratcheted up a few decibels. "All this land around and behind you is owned by me and my family. My land is right fucking behind you."

When his girlfriend would ask him later why they just didn't leave right then, he wouldn't be able to give her an intelligent answer. But something inside him—maybe the fight part of the fight-or-flight response, he couldn't be sure—made him question the white light, gun barrel, and black silhouette standing there. He would regret it, and have terrible sweat-soaked nightmares about it for many years to come.

"But you don't own the shoulder of the road. We're on the shoulder of the road. And this isn't a private road. It's Rural Route 14."

A muscular arm with a meat hook for a hand reached in and grabbed Lover Boy by the shirt collar. He twisted the cotton fabric so tightly Lover Boy could feel it constricting blood vessels and pinching skin. Before he could react, the other hand entered the vehicle and the barrel of the gun was stuffed into Lover Boy's mouth.

The woman opened her mouth to scream.

"I swear if I hear another fucking sound from you, Lover Boy over here is going to get his fucking face blown off."

She put her index finger in her mouth and bit hard on it to stifle the escaping sound. A tiny squeak emerged, followed by a long gasp.

Lover Boy's eyes were wide, his brow wrinkled in consternation.

The armed man addressed the wide eyes. "You ever talk back to me again, ever question my authority in this neck of the woods again, I'll blow your fucking head off." He stuffed the gun barrel an inch or so further into Lover Boy's mouth for emphasis. He emitted a slow gurgling sound.

"You hear me?"

Lover Boy nodded.

"You understand?"

He nodded.

"I'm going to remove this gun from your mouth. When I do, I want you to start your car and get the fuck out of here. And never come around my property again. You get the fuck out of here and don't say a fucking word to no one. You got that, Lover Boy?"

He nodded. The gun barrel slid out of his mouth and the car door was slammed shut with a reverberating clunk.

Lover Boy didn't even wait for his girlfriend to finish dressing, or climb into the front seat. He got into the driver's seat, and with a trembling hand started the motor. He shoulder-checked and pulled out slowly, careful not to spray his attacker with gravel. When he felt the tires rolling on asphalt, he instantly put pedal to metal and sped away, without immediately realizing the warm gush of liquid between his legs meant he had pissed his pants.

Chapter One

"I'm getting pissed."

"Why?"

"Look, there she goes again, driving by."

"Maybe she's got business in the area."

"What fucking business does she have checking our mailbox?" Dana Vilner said. She pushed the sheer blinds away from the window affording her a better view of the landlady driving away in the new green Ford Fiesta. The vehicle rounded a corner and disappeared out of sight before she turned her attention back to her boyfriend, Jackson LaPrairie, who by now had resumed packing. "Do you think she has business checking our mailbox? She did that yesterday. And do you think she has business knocking on the door three times in a day without proper notice? She did that yesterday too, you know."

"Okay, okay, she has no business other than to bug us." He adjusted his Toronto Blue Jays baseball cap sideways—that was how he sometimes wore it—picked up some newspaper, crunched it up, and pushed it into a cardboard box containing dishes. "But we're looking for a new place anyway, honey." It was followed by a loud chuckling laughter—bordering on a cackle—that rolled out of his mouth almost musically as he walked into the kitchen in search of more newspaper. That's what Jackson did in the face of stress—laugh. It was a coping mechanism. Some people cried. Others became angry, violent, depressed—at least a million other possibilities. Not Jackson. He laughed.

Dana wasn't laughing as she surveyed the scene in the living room. She hated moving. Didn't everyone? Along with death and divorce, it's said to be one of the top stress-triggers in the world. Cardboard boxes were strewn everywhere, along with miscellaneous items that would need to be packed. She wiped perspiration from her brow as she returned her gaze to the window, searching for landlady Vicki Chow. Vicki was nowhere to be seen.

Kid's toys littered the street of the run-down townhouse complex. A boy and girl no older than fifteen sat on a concrete porch directly across from her, drinking beer. They talked animatedly. Two doors down, six motley-looking characters with mullets drank beer on the front lawn and listened to a stereo thumping out heavy metal music.

Two kids ran into the street with a Frisbee and started tossing it.

It was mid-July, hot and muggy in the late-afternoon sun in Brantford, Ontario. The small, portable air conditioner in the living room window had coughed and sputtered a few hours earlier before spraying liquid all over the carpet. Dana had scrubbed the stain as best she could, but there was still a yellowish streak covering a portion of the well-worn beige carpet that was already soiled with black and brown dirt stains. Oh well. The carpet wasn't that clean when her family—Hillary, 14, Brittany, 19, black Lab Barney, 5, and of course the newest love in her life, Jackson, 45—had moved in just under three months ago.

She hadn't been there that long. And she hated moving. But, she wanted more than ever to leave.

The townhouse complex was a dump. Backing onto a main highway, the only good thing about it was its close proximity to downtown Brantford, inexpensive ($900 a month when comparably-sized units rented for $1,300 to $1,400 a month) and at 1,536 square feet, not including the undeveloped basement, it was large enough to accommodate her entire family.

But that was pretty much where it ended. The price attracted all the riff-raff you could imagine: disorderly kids, the result of little or no parental supervision, drug-addicts, criminals, party animals, couch potatoes and all manner of derelicts the human imagination was capable of conjuring up. It was no place to raise a family.

She had to get out of there.

The proverbial straw that broke the camel's back was Vicki. Due to an oversight, last month, Dana had bounced a rent check but quickly made good on the amount after Vicki had called and, in barely understandable English, explained the arrears. The next day Dana climbed in her blue pick-up truck and delivered another check to the woman.

That check *had* cleared.

But it was a few days after that Vicki began driving around the complex, peering out the window of her car, stalking the property and its inhabitants. Then a few impromptu visits without the proper twenty-four hour notice and two instances where Dana actually caught Vicki going through *her* mail. In *her* mailbox.

When she had confronted Vicki about the incidents, she was told the landlady was searching for another tenant's mail, which Vicki had promised to forward. To try and diffuse the situation, Dana had offered to kindly forward the mail to said tenant if Vicki would be so kind as to pass along the appropriate contact details.

Her offer was met with: "No, I do myself. My responsibility. None you business." And the Asian woman had quickly disappeared in her Fiesta.

So enough was enough, Dana thought. It was time to move on to greener pastures. She and Jackson had done some internet surfing last night and discovered that country houses rented for much cheaper ($700 to $800 per month), offered much more privacy and seclusion, and probably would provide a healthier environment to raise a family and deepen the bond in her one-year relationship with Jackson. And most of the country homes they saw were within a thirty-minute or so commute from Brantford.

They didn't need the riff-raff and the stress of a crazy landlady. They needed the peace, quiet and seclusion of the country. So, in anticipation of finding a home before the end of July, they had already started packing. Jackson had printed off five possibilities and they had four of them booked to see the next afternoon. If they found a place, they weren't planning to give Vicki a full month's notice. Her antics could probably be construed as harassment anyway. So, fuck her and the Fiesta she rode in on. At least that was Dana's opinion.

Dana stared out the window. But she was no longer seeing the riff-raff on the street winding up for another loud night of partying. Dana was lost in thought, thinking about an idyllic and peaceful life in the country. A place where she would have space to develop her airbrushing talents and Jackson would have the space to store his tools and expand his business as a construction contractor.

She caught her reflection in the window, and studied the face looking back at her. Long sandy-blonde hair, brown eyes, olive-toned skin and small facial features. She observed how the hard years had created dark black circles under her eyes, a few crow's feet that she no longer bothered to hide with make-up, and a worn-out look that disturbed her. *To hell with it. We all get old. For forty-five, I'm still pretty good-looking.* That was true. Dana's attractive features and shapely body still turned the heads of the neighborhood scumbags. Her long walks through the complex were often accompanied by a symphony of whistles and invites—which she politely ignored.

She was startled from her thoughts by the crunching of newspaper. Jackson had returned and begun packing. She could see his reflection in the window as he kneeled down in front of a box.

"Baby, are you still looking for Vicki?" Jackson's comment was followed by a chuckle.

She turned around, surveying her latest catch. Jackson was tall and lanky, just over six feet, with big brown eyes, a gaunt face, a crooked nose, long brown hair and an easy smile that displayed crooked, although very white, teeth. Like Dana, he grew up slightly above the poverty line. But Dana liked him for his easy disposition and irreverent sense of humor that matched her own. Sometimes, they would both end up rolling in hysterical laughter at the stupidest and most mundane comment.

"No, I'm dreaming about a life in paradise," she said, going into the kitchen. "Want a beer?"

"Sure. I thought this was paradise?"

She returned and handed him a Molson Canadian can. "If you think this is paradise, you've died and gone to hell."

"I guess I've died and gone to hell then." He opened the can with a loud click. It foamed over. He quickly put his mouth to it and sopped it up before it could drip on the already-beaten rug.

Maybe it was his odd expression as he peered at her while licking and sucking the escaping foam, or the familiar chortle when he finally brought the exploding can under control, but she couldn't help bursting into loud laughter.

When their laughter had subsided, Jackson eyeballed her beer and nodded. "Aren't you going to open it?"

Even though it would be funny, she wasn't prepared to repeat his performance. So she walked into the kitchen, held the can over the sink and popped it open. A fountain of white foam sprayed up and blasted her in the eyes and face. She quickly set the can down, backed away, and began wiping her dripping face.

Jackson's thunderous laughter echoed through the house. Barney ran into the living room and started barking playfully. Hillary and Brittany appeared in the stairwell. Seeing Jackson rolling around the carpet, the dog standing over him, barking, and Dana's face covered in white foam created another chorus of laughter from the girls.

"All right," Dana said good-naturedly, grabbing a towel and wiping away the last of the foam. "The show's over."

Then she looked at Jackson, mock-anger in her eyes. "You shook that can, didn't you?"

Jackson shook his head, but his eyes told a different story.

And Dana could read that story as clear as a bell. "You little shit," she said, charging into the living room, unable to contain a smile. "I'm going to kill you."

Chapter Two

"People don't kill unless they're predisposed to kill," Dana said.

"I'm not so sure about that," Jackson said. "What if they're backed into a corner?"

"What do you mean?"

"I mean, like if your life depended on it."

"What, like self-defense?"

"Yeah."

"That's different," Dana said. "I'm not talking about self-defense."

"What are you talking about?"

"Let's say someone really pisses me off, rips me off for a bunch of money, something like that. I wouldn't kill them over it. Nor would I beat the shit out of them."

"What if they killed or seriously maimed one of your kids?"

"I still wouldn't kill them."

"You don't know that."

"Yeah, I do."

"No, you don't. How can you know how you'll react in a situation that you've never been in before?"

"I'm just saying I wouldn't kill anyone over it. I'd go to the police."

"What if the police fucked up, the guy walked away?"

"I still wouldn't do anything."

"You don't know that."

"Yeah, I do. I believe in karma. What goes around comes around—which means he'd get his anyway, but it doesn't have to be from me."

"Don't you think revenge would be sweet?"

"I guess it would be, but I wouldn't be the one to do it."

"What, you'd hire someone?"

"No, I'd let karma take care of it."

"You can't say that unless you've actually been pushed into the situation. No one knows how they'd react unless they go through the experience. Everyone's capable of murder."

Dana paused, smoking her cigarette, gazing out the window of her pick-up truck as they rolled down a country road just outside Brantford. As the greenery, small farmsteads, the odd horse or field of cows whipped by her sight line, she wondered if Jackson had a point. If someone killed or injured one of her daughters, and they walked away scot-free, would she really let karma take its course?

She would certainly like to think she wouldn't act in an irrational way, but how did she really know how she would act if it never happened to her? She did know, however, that she didn't want to continue this discussion right now. They had just viewed three acreage properties advertised for rent and all were absolute dumps. On the last one, some crotchety old man had staggered out of his dilapidated house, aiming a double-barrel 12-gauge sawed-off shotgun at them, shouting, "Get the fuck off my property unless you want your head blown off."

They discovered a little while later they had the wrong address. Acreages were hard to find at the best of times, even worse without the aid of a GPS.

They eventually spotted the small acreage less than a quarter mile away but their experience with shit-faced shot-gun man had prompted them to cancel the appointment and move further north about ten miles to the last house on the list.

"Well, I'll tell you something," Jackson said, lighting a smoke in the passenger seat. "If that old fuck would have killed you and got off, I'd be awfully tempted to kill him."

Dana glanced over at Jackson, who had a silly little grin on his face. She didn't know if she wanted to offer him any encouragement, but had to admit she was flattered by the veiled declaration of love and loyalty. "I appreciate that, baby. But could we resume this conversation another time? We're almost there."

"No problem."

She turned onto Rural Route 14, a narrow two-lane highway, and looked for the signs landlady Gertrude Sebastian had told her would become visible about a quarter mile after the turn-off.

"There," she said a few minutes later. She turned down the long gravel driveway, bordered by large maple trees and smaller brush, which completely concealed the two-story house from the road. *Nice and private. Just what we're looking for.*

The property sat on five nicely treed acres with a well-manicured lawn and an oversized double detached garage. It would be perfect for her to do airbrushing and perfect for Jackson to ply his carpenter trade. A wood and wire fence bordered the property and there was a small pond that looked ideal for swimming a little ways down a gently sloping hill. The house itself was grey wood siding with large, white-trimmed windows. For a rental property, it looked reasonably well-maintained.

They noticed a small blue four-door sedan parked in the driveway, but there was no one around.

It was hot and muggy. Dana pulled a napkin from the glove box and wiped her sweaty brow while Jackson fumbled for the camera and started snapping photos.

"Looks like a nice place for a swim," she said, pointing to the pond.

He nodded. "Want to go for a dip?"

"We don't have the place yet."

They exited the vehicle and heard the front door creak open. A plump woman in her mid-sixties, wearing blue polyester pants, a black t-shirt, white flip-flops, approached and greeted them with a warm smile. "I'm Gertrude." She extended a hand. She had short, thick greyish-brown hair, small horn-rimmed glasses, a pudgy face, and beady brown eyes. Her face was dripping with perspiration.

They finished with introductions and Gertrude produced a white linen handkerchief, removed her glasses, and mopped the sweat from her face. "Awfully hot out," she said, smiling. She replaced her glasses and led them into the house. As they stepped on the porch, she pointed to the pond. "Feel free to take a swim in there anytime. If things work out, that is."

As they toured the interior, which was clean and reasonably well-maintained, Gertrude asked questions. "How many kids do you have?"

"I have two daughters, fourteen and nineteen," Dana said.

"Any pets?"

"A black Lab. Very friendly and well-trained."

"How long have you been with Jackson?"

"A year."

"You guys don't fight?"

"No. The odd tiff now and again, which is normal. But we're happy together."

"And what about work?"

"I do airbrushing. Motorcycle paint jobs, murals, custom work."

"How long have you been doing that?"

"Six years."

"Things going well?"

Dana nodded.

Gertrude turned to Jackson. "What kind of work do you do?"

"I'm a construction contractor."

And on and on it went until they went outside to the garage. It was a wooden structure with peeling paint and shingles missing from the roof. Opening the double wood doors, Dana saw the pool of water collecting on one of the tarps that covered some furniture and other items inside.

"This leaks," she said, frowning.

"We need to do a few repairs," Gertrude said.

"Does the garage come with the house?"

Gertrude nodded.

"We need a place by the end of July," Dana said. "But we need a garage to run our businesses. Will this be ready by then?"

"Oh yes," Gertrude said with a plastic smile. "We'll fix the roof and get rid of all that stuff in a week."

"It sounds good," Jackson said, beaming a crooked smile. "What do you think, honey?"

Dana nodded. "Is there an application or something that we can get from you?"

"For sure," Gertrude said. "Let's go back into the house. You'll find this area really great. The neighbors are wonderful and it's so quiet and peaceful here."

"That's what we're hoping for," Dana said as they walked. "Peace and quiet."

As they were leaving, Dana said: "One more thing I should tell you. Our landlady in Brantford had been going through our mail, actually stalking our property. Although we're paid up, if you talk to her, I don't think she'll give us a very good reference. But those other references will check out."

Gertrude frowned slightly, scratching her head. "Stalking you? Why would she do that?"

"You know how it goes," Dana said. "It takes all kinds of people to make the world go round."

Chapter Three

"Go around, you fucking cocksucker," Jackson shouted out the open window of the pick-up truck as he slowed down and watched the vehicle barreling straight toward him on Rural Route 14. He couldn't identify the make of it, but he could see it was grey and coming awfully fast.

"You mean, stay in your own lane," Dana said, her eyes growing wider.

"Yeah, whatever. He started off in his lane, but look, he's in our lane now."

It happened about two minutes after pulling out from the potential rental property. They had just started to discuss first impressions of Gertrude Sebastian. Jackson figured she would be fair and reasonable to deal with, while Dana had a nagging feeling—and she couldn't put her finger on the reason why—that the woman would be trouble.

"Well, pull over to the shoulder and let the nut-job pass," Dana said.

The oncoming grey truck was perhaps two city blocks away now, in their lane, and accelerating.

Jackson felt the adrenaline surging, that illogical blast of power that enables a person to do all manner of smart, stupid, or brave things in the face of imminent danger. Some people have been known to completely black out; others have committed violent and heinous crimes while under its forceful buzz. Others—if they choose flight over fight—might flee in terror or turn to alcoholism, drug abuse, even prolonged bouts watching television as catatonic couch potatoes. Wallowing in avoidance, thinking it would make all their problems disappear.

What would Jackson do?

"Fuck him. Let him get back in his proper lane." He kept the truck steady, even increased the speed marginally and bee-lined it right for the oncoming vehicle.

Dana's eyes were wide with fear, and she felt a surge of adrenaline. "You don't know who you're dealing with. Pull over into the ditch!"

Jackson glanced at Dana, his face flushed red, eyes wide and bulging in their sockets. He gripped the wheel, white-knuckled.

The vehicles were now perhaps a hundred and fifty feet from each other, and neither driver was willing to back down from the impromptu game of chicken. You could call it a pissing contest, but Jackson felt his bowels loosen, like he was about to shit his pants at any second.

He opened his mouth to speak, but before he could utter a single sound, Dana yelled: "PULL THIS FUCKING TRUCK INTO THE DITCH RIGHT NOW!"

Jackson jerked the wheel, slowed down, and slammed on the brakes. The truck was going much too fast. It skidded on the hot pavement, the tires screeching. The ass-end skidded out into the left lane momentarily before he brought the fishtailing under control and drove into the weed-infested ditch, slamming the front bumper hard into dirt as the momentum carried them halfway up the other side.

The grey vehicle, an older Dodge Ram pick-up truck, slowed as it passed the ditch. The man behind the wheel had no intention of helping the accident victims. Instead, he threw his left arm out the window, pointed his forefinger and thumb like a handgun, cocked an eyebrow, adjusted his black Molson Canadian baseball cap down, and sped away.

It was all Dana could do to flip him the bird and yell, "Fuck off."

Chapter Four

"Fuck off ... and fuck you and the piece of shit truck you rolled in on," Gord Sebastian, the forty-six-year-old son of Gertrude Sebastian, said to himself as he drove down Rural Route 14 and watched the ditched pick-up become a tiny dot in his rearview mirror. As much as he had just felt he had gotten the better of the last game of chicken, he still wasn't particularly pleased with his efforts.

He should have gotten out of the truck and pummeled the shit out of the two, whoever they were, for daring to drive on Rural Route 14 near his property.

But abruptly the aching in the back of his head reminded him that perhaps he would have to be a bit more subtle in his intimidation. He scratched the brownish-grey stubble on his chin, tucked a few locks of his thick mop of curly brown hair under the cap, and rubbed the goose-egg on the back of his head. It smarted and he removed his hand quickly. It was still almost grapefruit-sized, even though he had received the surprise gift three days ago.

For the last two years, he had been engaged in a turf war of sorts with his neighbors, Hank and Rebecca Sault. They were a retired couple who owned five acres with a couple of outbuildings just off Rural Route 14, about a mile from Gord's acreage. In their late sixties, they were happy to help out their neighbors—at least the ones they felt weren't psychotic—and had a few close friends in the community whom they visited or would have over infrequently.

For the most part, they were happy with their own company, their thirty-year marriage, and their hobbies. It was one such hobby that eventually steered Hank straight into a dangerous path with Gord. Hank liked taking his SUV out at night, driving alone along the peaceful and scenic country roads, while his wife watched television, read, whatever piqued her fancy. They both understood they needed time by themselves once in a while. It was one of the things that had kept them happy in their marriage for so many years.

But Gord took exception to Hank driving by at what he said were "odd hours."

Hank didn't share that opinion. His thinking was that if he felt like taking a drive in the country at 10:00 pm—the usual time for sojourns—well, then that was his and maybe his wife's business only. Nobody else's.

So, he was irritated when Gord started speeding by him on the highway during these nightly excursions, dangling out the universally-understood index finger greeting. In fact, old Hank was even less impressed when Gord dropped over uninvited, speeding down the long, winding gravel driveway to his acreage mid-afternoon on three separate occasions. On one such visit, Gord abruptly stopped the truck, exited, and asked Hank to "limit your outings to respectable day-time hours."

On all three visits, Hank had barely said a word to his not-so-neighborly neighbor.

For Hank it was the fourth visit that triggered the fight-or-flight response. And it wasn't flight.

High on crack-cocaine, weed, and a dozen Molson Canadian beers, Gord had the bright idea to accost Hank early in the evening while Hank was tending to his vegetable garden, turning up weeds with a large spade.

Gord had skidded onto the shoulder of the road, exited his pick-up truck in a rage, yelling and screaming. "Why don't you listen to me when I tell you your engine noise bothers me?"

Hank calmly stopped his weeding, listened to about five minutes of ranting and raving, nodding his head, a small smirk barely visible. Finally, exhausted from his outburst, Gord turned to leave. It was then that Hank raised the shovel, cocking it like Albert Pujols about to score one of many homeruns, and hammered Gord so hard on the back of the head he hit the ground like a sledgehammer.

Hank calmly went into his house, cracked open a can of Molson Canadian—a tribute to the baseball cap that had flown off Gord's head on impact—took a long pull, and grinned ear-to-ear.

Of course, Gord wasn't grinning when he woke up about four hours later in a prickly cucumber patch. No. He might have initially thought it was the attack of the killer cucumbers that were responsible for his unintended slumber. But when his head finally cleared, he realized his face-plant in a vegetable garden had nothing to do with killer cucumbers. No. Hank had finally heard enough and seen red.

Picking himself off of prickly cucumber vines, Gord had a good mind to return to his truck, retrieve the trusty Glock, enter the house and murder the man who had severely concussed and almost killed him. But, truth be told, he was too dazed and confused to bother. It would have to wait until he felt better. It was all he could do to stagger to his truck, which was out of gas. Gord had left the vehicle idling during what he thought would be a brief but enjoyable episode of intimidation. He hadn't realized he had pushed this otherwise gentle giant well past the boiling point.

He retrieved his cell phone and called his crack-cocaine-addicted buddy, Bruce Hammerstein, to come to the rescue.

And that little miscalculation left him sitting in the truck for another hour, fuming, while Bruce—at his own leisurely and wasted pace—finally retrieved a gas can and some gas and rescued him.

Gord pulled into his acreage and wondered when he would take revenge on Hank. So far, it seemed a shovel to the back of the head was one of the few things that Gord listened to these days. It was an action that spoke much louder than words.

Bruce stuck his gaunt, weathered face out from under the hood of a beat-up green 1966 Ford Falcon he was fixing, tossed a wrench on the ground, extracted two Molson Canadian beers from a nearby cooler, and offered one to Gord as he exited his truck.

With furrowed uni-brow and a look of consternation pointing the corners of his thin lips down, Gord regarded his friend, his beady brown eyes searching for a chord of discontent in the flippant demeanor of Bruce. *If he says anything remotely sarcastic, I'm going to let him have it.*

But all Bruce did was offer a toothy grin and hand over a beer. Gord accepted it. Bruce's pupils were already dilated, even though it was mid-afternoon, hot and sunny. Bruce had already been smoking crack, which came as no surprise to Gord.

They had a deal. Bruce would repair cars around Gord's acreage in exchange for money to buy crack and a roof over his head. Among the outbuildings, which included a large shop and an even larger barn, there was a run-down trailer behind some brush that was home-sweet-home to Bruce. After the cars were fixed, Gord had a wholesale connection in Brantford, Ralph Nadaport, to whom he would sell the cars. Gord had thought about retailing the vehicles himself, but he had started to realize his people skills weren't exactly impeccable. Besides, he didn't want every Tom, Dick and Harry parading out to his acreage to view vehicles. It was much easier to sell them to Ralph and let Ralph deal with the public.

Gord had a hard enough time dealing with Bruce. If it wasn't for Bruce's mechanical skills, Gord probably would have punted him down the road long ago. But, hell, Bruce was cheap labor, generated a little drug money at times, and gave Gord someone to talk to, belittle, and boss around.

Gord cracked open his beer, took a long pull, and regarded his friend. He used the term "friend" loosely. "How's the car coming?"

Bruce removed his grease-stained baseball cap that showed a hint of red, its former color prior to being saturated with grime. He raked a dirty hand over an unkempt mop of sandy brown hair, opened his beer, and drank before speaking. "Needs a new starter. And the battery's fried."

There was a junk heap of wrecks scattered around the shop, a few more rusting in a metal graveyard beside the barn. Gord waved his hand at the wrecks. "Can you recycle anything from those?"

"There's a pick-up truck that might have a battery, but I'm pretty sure we need a new starter, boss."

"I'll deal with it tomorrow," Gord said, gingerly walking toward the Falcon. He peered under the hood, scratching his nuts and wincing in pain.

Bruce noticed the discomfort. "What happened to you?"

"Horseback riding a few days ago. My nuts still hurt."

"What happened?"

"There was something wrong with the stirrups and the horse was some wild bucking bronco."

"Why'd you pick such a wild horse?"

"I didn't. The horse handler ... cowboy did."

"You say anything to piss him off?"

"I told him I thought he looked like a fruitcake." Gord thought for a minute. "Come to think of it, after that he switched horses on me. Said the one I was supposed to ride suddenly had a heart palpitation ... said he had a better one. There was something wrong with the stirrups, too. They didn't fit right. Every time the horse jumped I would come down hard on my nuts. I'll never ride another horse again for as long as I live."

Bruce knew better than to say too much. He was cognizant of Gord's explosive temper. But, he thought, pushing the envelope a little wouldn't hurt. "Why'd you call him a fruitcake?"

"Because he was one."

"Couldn't you have waited until after the ride was over?"

"Maybe I should have."

"Yeah ... sounds like he jury-rigged the stirrups and gave you a wild horse just to fuck you up."

"I'll fucking kill that bastard next time I see him."

"How bad are your nuts?"

"I still got a lot of bruising. And that was two days ago. I had to ice my nuts when I got home, and two days later, I still feel it."

"What did the cowboy say when you got back?"

Gord thought about the two cowboys loudly guffawing with laughter as he slowly dismounted the stud, doubled over, grabbed his nuts, and gingerly left the stable.

His eyes narrowed and he balled his fists. "Enough already." He turned and walked toward his two-story home, absently rubbing his groin. "Get some fucking work done. I've got shit to do."

Bruce bit his lip and waited patiently until he heard the door close before he doubled over, ducked behind one of the wrecks, rolled in the grass and squealed like a pig; but not because his nuts were sore.

Chapter Five

"Are you fucking nuts?" Dana asked Jackson two days later as they sat in the backyard in the early evening, drinking beer in their Brantford townhouse.

Jackson had just told her that Gertrude called and said their application for tenancy at the Rural Route 14 acreage had been accepted. She wanted to see them the following evening to do an inspection of the property, collect first and last month's rent, and sign a lease for July 31st. Jackson had indicated that they were probably interested, but he would confirm it with his girlfriend and call her back shortly. In spite of the near-death experience during the impromptu game of vehicular chicken, and Dana's bad vibe about Gertrude, Jackson was leaning toward renting the property. And he was trying to urge Dana on board.

"I have nuts," Jackson said. "Some people even call them stones ... balls for sure. But no, I'm not nuts." He laughed.

In spite of herself, Dana smiled. But she still wasn't sure about renting the property. "You mean to tell me that after we almost get killed leaving the place, you want to move in there? We could be going from bad to worse."

The situation with landlady Vicki Chow had become untenable. Her stalking had become more frequent, and there was a water leak under the bathroom sink that was slowly rotting wood and drywall, creating mold. When asked about it, Vicki had unceremoniously declared: "That kind of thing is you responsibility."

Dana didn't share that opinion. And she didn't like exposing her kids to mold. Nor did she like the looks she had been getting from both of her daughters lately as they noticed her stress level rising. Of course, she had refrained from telling them she and Jackson had almost been killed while looking for a new home for the family, but other comments had slipped out that they *had* heard. Her youngest, Hillary, had come down into the living room recently in the middle of the night and asked her mom if they were going to be all right.

"Of course we are," was all Dana had managed. She had hugged Hillary and sent her to bed. But then thoughts had swirled around in her mind about their precarious financial situation, the need for more space to ply their respective trades, and how prohibitively expensive it would be to try to arrange a commercial lease space. A country property with a large shop was perfect, especially at $850 per month. And they had yet to find anything remotely as good in terms of physical condition and price.

"I don't know how much worse we can get than this place," Jackson wondered, glancing a few doors down at a crew of local riff-raff beginning what was sure to be a long and raucous party. As if on cue, a mangy-looking guy flipped him the one-finger salute, laughed, drained his beer, tossed the empty onto the grass and went inside.

Watching the discourteous loser, Dana bit her tongue. She was beginning to acquiesce. "Maybe you're right."

There was a long pause while she thought. In the last three years, they had averaged four apartments a year. Disagreements with landlords, roaches for landlords. But, she had to admit, financial difficulty, relationship strife, injuries and lack of funds—on her part—had also played a role in the game of musical houses. One every four months. That was a lot. And how many boyfriends had she gone through in the last three years. Was it one a year? She thought so. A little better, but not much. She wondered at what point she could stop calling herself a victim and begin claiming some responsibility for the trail of misery and calamity in her past.

And what about the kids? What effect was it having on them? Hillary had been acting out aggression and disrespect for authority for the last five years. It had only been this year that she had matured, and realized with all the problems Dana was having, she certainly didn't need any more. Hillary knew her attitude wasn't helping matters, and Dana was doing the best she knew how. So, she had stopped acting out and gradually become more respectful.

Brittany could have turned out a lot worse. Standing five-foot-seven, with short brown hair, brown eyes, a quirky smile and round face with pudgy cheeks, she didn't contribute much around the house, but was generally respectful and well-behaved, if a reclusive and anti-social teenager. She rarely went out, had one or two good friends, and spent most of her time on the internet, doing what nineteen-year-old kids do on the internet—post and play on Facebook.

Recently, the family doctor had mentioned to Dana that Brittany was suffering from depression and if it continued, a referral to a psychiatrist and a possible regiment of anti-depressants might be in order.

And the last thing Dana wanted was for her daughter to be on anti-depressants. Way back in her family tree, there had been some mental illness. She prayed to God that the pattern would not continue with her offspring. Up until now, it hadn't.

Dana also thought that in Jackson, she had finally found a man whom she could stay with for the rest of her life. Truth be told, his past wasn't a great improvement from hers. But at least he was honest, treated them with love and respect, was loyal to a fault and had a positive attitude that seemed to brighten every room he entered. In spite of his tumultuous past, he still viewed the bowl of cherries as half full. And Dana, with next to no family support, needed that positive influence and support in her life now more than ever.

Besides, she loved him.

"I'm waiting for your wheels to stop turning," he said. "Whenever your eyes go like that, I know you're kicking everything around."

"I don't know what to do," she said finally. The pressure was mounting from all sides.

"Why don't we try it, honey?"

They clinked beer cans and kissed. Resuming her seat in the plastic lawn chair, Dana smiled and said: "We better make this work, Jackson, or I'll kick you in the ass."

Chapter Six

A kick in the ass, Seth thought as he trudged out to the barn to retrieve his red Budweiser baseball cap. *Another kick in the ass.* Looking much more haggard than his seventy-four years might suggest, Gertrude Sebastian's husband had forgotten to bring his baseball cap back inside the house for dinner after he had spent the afternoon cleaning and organizing the barn, which now doubled as a garage for the couple's multitude of farm implements, tools and vehicles.

And Gertrude, who had a special hook inside the mudroom for every hat that Seth owned—and there were fifteen in total—wanted to see the hat back in its rightful place, not "scattered haphazardly somewhere in the barn," as she had quickly pointed out when he entered to eat dinner. So she had ordered him back out to retrieve the hat "before you set foot inside this kitchen."

He opened the white man-door to the freshly-painted red barn, flicked the overhead fluorescents and stood blinking while his eyes adjusted to the light. It took a few minutes of wandering around the gargantuan space, but eventually his tired eyes fell on a stack of blue Tupperware storage bins. There it was, sitting on top of one of them. He picked it up, scratched his bald head (he had thick gray hair that would only grow on the sides and back) and put it on. *What was the first kick in the ass? Oh yeah, marrying her. No, today, we're talking.*

Then he remembered. He had planned on spending a leisurely day painting in the loft area of the barn until Gertrude had ordered him to "clean up your act out there before you lift

37

another paintbrush." That was the other kick in the ass. At least today's tally, anyway.

Seth would never be a famous artist. It was just a hobby. But he found refuge and therapy in creating scenic landscapes in oil paint, sometimes to escape the tyranny of his marriage. He had also dabbled in watercolors, and, glancing at one of his latest paintings hanging in the barn, a hodge-podge of splashes—blacks, grays, browns—speckled with little white drops, he couldn't help but notice how his precise style of old had given way to wilder and bolder strokes. Aggressive and grim could also be interpreted in the contemporary abstracts, he thought.

He sighed deeply, turned the lights out and returned to the house. Gertrude was busy in the kitchen as he approached the kitchen sink.

"How many times do I have to tell you not to wash your hands in there? Use the bathroom. That's what it's for."

Third kick in the ass.

As he walked down the hall, the door opened and Gord entered, still treading gingerly. "Hi Mom. Hey, old man. How's everything?"

Seth waved and proceeded to the bathroom while Gord kissed Gertrude on the lips and proceeded to wash his hands in the kitchen sink.

A few minutes later, they sat down to dinner. Gertrude served up steak, mashed potatoes and corn.

Seth cut into his steak and frowned slightly, realizing it was well-done. He liked it rare.

"Just how I like it," Gord said, waving a bite-sized morsel of steak around with his fork, the blood-red inside clearly visible. It was rare.

She beamed with delight.

Seth turned to his son. "You haven't been getting into any trouble, have you?"

Gertrude bristled. "He's a good boy, Seth. He doesn't get into trouble."

"What happened to your head?" Seth asked, ignoring the reproach. "Lose an argument with a baseball bat?" He didn't know how close to the truth he had come.

"No," Gord said after a tense silence. "I was fixing a hood on a car and it slammed down on me."

"You should get that looked at, boy," Gertrude said, leaping up and examining the goose-egg.

"Leave it, Mom. It hurts. And I don't need a doctor."

She sat down, said nothing, and continued eating.

After a moment's silence, Gertrude said, "It looks like we have some new tenants moving into the house down the road."

Gord raised an eyebrow. "New tenants? I thought we were going to subdivide that acreage and sell it."

"We will eventually, honey, but we're going to rent it for a couple of years first."

A frown creased Gord's features. "I don't want any neighbors."

"Well, if you see them doing anything unusual, tell me and we'll straighten them out in a hurry."

"What, like you did with the last tenants?" Seth asked between mouthfuls of mashed potatoes. The last tenants had pulled a midnight move, claiming that a new rule was being imposed every day and it had become too invasive to their well-being and privacy. Finally, after Gertrude had strategically placed *NO TRESPASSING* signs around the perimeter of the acreage, the young family with three small children decided enough was enough. They packed up their belongings and spray-painted on the white living room wall, just because they could—*THIS IS THE HOUSE OF HARRASSMENT*—and disappeared.

They had lasted a day under two months.

"We'll see," Gertrude said. Then, after a short pause: "Maybe it would be a good idea for you to meet Dana and Jackson tomorrow?"

Seth knew it wasn't a question. It was a statement, irrefutable. But he tried anyway. "I was hoping to do some painting tomorrow." Once a mechanical engineer for an oil company, Seth was not-so-happily retired, but at least he didn't have to worry about money. The couple owned hundreds of acres in the area, leased much of it to farmers, and had even gifted twenty acres and a house to their son—for his loyalty and obedience.

The only job Gord ever had in his entire lifetime was a short stint as a long-haul trucker. That had lasted six months before he decided his boss, who was always telling him what to do, would look much better with a knuckle sandwich. Evidently the boss didn't like his reflection in the mirror with two front teeth missing. He had fired Gord and pressed charges for assault—which were later dropped, the result of a hefty bribe.

Now Gord owned twenty acres clear title, and his parents gave him a $2,000 monthly allowance, profits from their many investments. For that, he was told to keep an eye on the hundreds of acres the family owned. He took his job very seriously.

"You can do your painting once you finish with them," Gertrude insisted.

What the hell, Seth thought. Gertrude had a miserable track record when it came to dealing with people—with the exception of the pride and joy sitting in front of her, chewing his steak with an open mouth, slurping sounds echoing through the expansive kitchen.

Maybe Seth could do a better job?

Chapter Seven

"Maybe you can get a better job," Jackson said as Dana pulled the pick-up truck into the Safeway parking lot. They were going to buy some snacks and drinks before they embarked on their trip to what would eventually become their new home. They had decided to leave the girls and the dog at home.

Their conversation, as it often had lately, turned to money. More specifically, the lack thereof.

"Maybe I can," Dana said. Along with her fledgling airbrushing business, she also did home care for two seniors. But the job was only part-time, and didn't pay well. "And maybe I can get the airbrushing business fired up once we get settled out there. They said we can use the garage."

She pulled into a parking spot and killed the ignition.

Jackson nodded. "That's true. And it'll be a lot easier for me to do contracting with a garage." Occasionally, his work called for him to build things from wood and deliver them to jobsites. But the small single garage in their current complex didn't offer a lot of room. It was stuffed to the rafters with Dana's airbrushing equipment and other miscellaneous junk. There was barely enough room for Dana to work. And, without proper ventilation, it was hardly a suitable space to paint motorcycle gas tanks.

Jackson noticed four kids—probably in their early twenties—huddled together, smoking a joint in the parking lot. The tallest of the group, who had a mop of wild black hair, glared at Jackson as he exited the truck. Blackhead handed the joint to a friend and approached Jackson. "Did you say something to me?"

From the driver side of the vehicle, Dana watched the scene unfold.

"What?" Jackson said, his eyes widening. By this time, Blackhead was standing a few feet away, a menacing expression contorting his already ugly features.

"You heard me. You called me a name."

"No I didn't. I was talking with my girlfriend."

By this time, Blackhead's three friends had encircled Jackson.

"That's fucking bullshit and you know it." Blackhead's eyes narrowed and he clenched his fists, a large vein bulging and pulsating on his forehead. His friends continued to smoke the joint, their features brightening.

Ringside seats.

Jackson backed up. He could smell alcohol on Blackhead's breath. Out of the corner of his eye, he saw it suddenly—a fist, over the top, angling straight for his head. He stepped back and the swing missed. "What the hell are you doing? I didn't provoke any of this. I don't want to fight you."

"Get the hell out of here," Dana shouted. "We're trying to go shopping."

The circle of three laughed. Blackhead ignored the comment and swung wildly at Jackson's head. Jackson jerked his head back and the punch missed.

Jackson's face flushed red. He wanted to fight. But on a rational level, he understood that he was outnumbered; it was best   not   to   provoke   this   confrontation   into   a knock-down-drag-out brawl even though it was rapidly escalating out of his control.

Blackhead swung again. Jackson ducked and the rapid roundhouse punch struck the fender hard with a metallic clang.

Thinking about it later, Dana realized it was just dumb luck that two pedal-bike cops rolled around the corner. Otherwise, she and Jackson probably would have gotten the shit kicked out of them.

"Help ... help ... help us, please!" she shouted. Both officers heard the cry and quickly pedaled over.

A man in the circle of three swallowed the burning joint. Blackhead stepped back into the group, rubbing the knuckles on his right hand, trying to conceal a wince.

"He assaulted us," Dana said, pointing at Blackhead, who was now beginning to walk away with his cronies.

"Hold it right there, boys," one of the cops said. They stopped moving and he pedaled toward them, a good thirty feet away from where Jackson and Dana stood.

The other cop pedaled his bike over to Jackson and Dana. He introduced himself as Constable Lorenzo Sealing. He had a black moustache, sharp brown eyes, an olive-toned complexion and perfectly aligned white teeth. His brown hair was cut short, slightly longer than a crew-cut.

"What happened here?" he asked.

"That guy over there started swinging at me for no reason," Jackson said. He eyes were intent, even scared.

"Which guy?"

"The tallest one, with the green t-shirt, long black hair."

His partner was talking to the group of four just out of earshot.

"Swinging at you? What trying to punch you?"

"Yeah."

"What'd you do to provoke that?"

"Nothing. We stopped here to get some groceries and they accosted us."

"Did he hit you?"

"No, I ducked."

"Stay here a minute, will you?"

"Sure."

Sealing pedaled over to the group. Dana and Jackson waited while he had a short discussion with them.

He returned. "They say they did nothing of the sort, that you started mouthing off, yelling profanities at them, and all they were doing was giving you a piece of their mind in retaliation."

"That's bullshit," Jackson said.

"That is bullshit," Dana said.

There was a moment's pause as Sealing regarded Dana and Jackson. Finally, he said, "Do you want to press charges?"

Jackson knew better than to enter rat territory. In Brantford, rats not only didn't thrive, but they generally got black-balled, and got the shit kicked out of them. And that was on the streets—never mind when they entered the prison system.

He shook his head. Dana shook her head.

"Well, then go your own separate way. I'll make sure they do the same."

He started to pedal away and stopped abruptly, calling the two, who had begun walking toward the Safeway supermarket. "One more thing."

Dana turned around. "What?"

"Try and look after yourselves, will you? I'm not your babysitter, you know."

Dana was about to say something about cops being the protector of law and order, but Jackson grabbed her by the arm. "Don't waste your breath. Let's go." He chuckled—the signature laugh had returned.

A short time later, they rolled along the highway, munching on Doritos and drinking Coke. They were quiet as Dana drove, occasionally glancing out the windows and enjoying the scenic countryside and rolling hills of Ontario.

Eventually they pulled onto Rural Route 14. It was half past eight and the orange sun was setting in the distance, partially obscured by a thick blanket of gray-black clouds.

Dana watched the white lights of a lone oncoming vehicle approaching and couldn't help getting flashbacks of the vehicle that had almost killed them a few days earlier. It had sped away so fast—and she had been so terrified—she hadn't gotten a good look at it. Neither had Jackson. Somewhere in her mind was the image of a gray half-ton pick-up truck. But now it was all a blur. They hadn't bothered to report anything to the police. Without a vehicle description, what were they supposed to tell the cops? And after the last experience with Sealing, Dana was no longer interested. Besides, she didn't trust cops much anyway.

When it was within a hundred or so feet, the oncoming vehicle switched its high-beams on. Dana was in no mood for jokes and followed suit. But instead of playing chicken, the vehicle—now she did see that it was a dark-colored pick-up truck—accelerated rapidly and roared passed them.

Jackson craned his neck as it passed.

"Is that the same vehicle that tried to run us off the road?" she asked.

"I don't know. I didn't see it that well."

"I think it was a gray pick-up." But she wasn't sure. And it didn't matter now. They had arrived at the rental property. They drove down the long driveway and parked in front of the house. Seth exited and greeted them with handshakes. Introductions were exchanged.

"Where's Gertrude?" Dana asked as they walked into the house.

"She had some other business to attend to. She asked me to handle it."

As they walked up the small porch, Dana heard the faint roar of an engine on the highway fronting the property. The tree-line and brush concealed the vehicle. She could only see headlights twinkling through the trees and hear the sound of the motor decelerating. Was it stopping in front of the house? She thought so.

She decided to ignore it for now, wanting more than ever to get the lease signed, then get the hell home to a cold beer—or if she felt like it, maybe a joint.

As they walked through the house, Seth pointed to stairs leading to the three bedrooms. The brown stairs were scuffed and dirty, as were the walls. What was once white paint was now tinted a yellowish-brown. Nicotine stains. The previous tenants had been heavy smokers.

"We're going to paint the stairs and the walls there," Seth said. "Before you move in."

"You don't have to do that," Jackson offered.

Dana pinched his arm hard. "That would be good, if you can get it done."

"We will," Seth assured them as Jackson rubbed the red spot on his forearm.

After touring the house, they went into the kitchen to sign the paperwork.

"Can we see the garage one more time?" Dana asked. "Before we sign anything."

Seth adjusted his blue Toronto Blue Jays baseball cap, scratched the gray stubble on his chin and stared at her confusedly. He was thinking about the cap and its rightful hook in the mudroom. He better not forget to hang it up when he returned home. *Another kick in the ass.*

"The garage?"

"Yeah," Dana said. "Gertrude said it was included in the lease. It's included, isn't it?"

After a short pause. "Yes, it is."

"Could we see it?"

"Sure."

They stepped off the wooden porch and walked across the lawn toward the garage. The sky was a bluish-gray haze, a small portion of the orange sunset barely visible as it crested over some trees in the distant horizon.

Through the tree-line, headlights twinkled.

"Do you know whose car that is on the road?" Dana asked, pointing at the grayish-white spheres of light poking through.

Seth stopped and adjusted his horn-rimmed spectacles. "No. Sometimes couples stop to ... you know, kiss along the road here. That's probably all it is. I wouldn't worry about it."

Dana wasn't convinced, but for the time being decided to ignore it. But she felt goose bumps crawl along her arms, and the hairs on the back of her neck stood up so straight it felt like they were piercing through the yellow halter-top she wore.

Seth pulled open a large door and flicked a switch. Two small incandescent lights illuminated the same pile of tarped debris and items they had seen earlier.

"We need this stuff gone before we move in," Dana said.

"I have lots of tools that I want in here," Jackson said. "And I have some cabinets for a client I need to build right away."

Seth nodded slowly. "We'll take care of it before you move in. I promise."

"Whose stuff is this?" Dana asked.

"I think it's a previous tenant's."

"They didn't bother to take it?"

"Guess not."

"Do you have legal possession of it?"

"I think so."

"But you'll get rid of it before we move in, right?"

"Yes, I will. Even if I have to get my son to take it with his truck, it'll be gone."

"You have a son?" Dana asked.

"Yes."

"He a good kid?"

As Seth paused, the vehicle's engine—parked just outside the tree-line—roared to life and it sped away, trailed by the screeching of tires. Seth winced at the sound.

Finally, he said, "He's not a kid anymore. He's in his forties."

The noise of the vehicle speeding away distracted Dana and she didn't realize that Seth had evaded the part of the question related to Seth's son's moral fiber.

"Let's get this paperwork completed," Seth said.

They returned to the house, signed a one-year lease, the inspection report, handed over first and last month's rent in cash, and left. They would be moving in ten days, on July 31st.

As they rolled down Rural Route 14, Dana couldn't help but wonder if they had made a bad decision. Something about Seth's spaced-out demeanor—and the pick-up truck seemingly stalking their every move—had spooked her yet again.

Forget about it. Put it out of your mind and enjoy your new country paradise.

Chapter Eight

"Is this paradise?" Hillary asked ten days later as they rolled down the driveway to their new home in the intense mid-afternoon heat. Jackson was driving a few minutes behind with Brittany in his 1998 silver Toyota Camry. They were charged with picking up a few grocery items. They planned on having Kentucky Fried Chicken and a few drinks to celebrate.

"Yes it is, honey," Dana said, nodding tentatively. She had met with Seth earlier at a Tim Horton's coffee shop in Brantford to retrieve the keys. The entire family had gotten up at 6:00 am to begin the new move and, as moves go, it hadn't gone all that badly. They had a U-Haul cube van with most of their stuff still packed sitting on the front lawn, and some belongings in their vehicles.

Dana had been disappointed when Seth said they hadn't gotten around to painting the stairs or stairwell. Seth wanted Dana and Jackson to do it, but quickly offered to pay for the paint.

Dana had nodded at the request, but couldn't help feeling how unfair it was. What happened to asking? Was that how these people were? They just *wanted* you to do things, like an order or something?

Under stress from the move and the frantic days leading up to it, Dana had decided to take a cup of shut the fuck up. So she sipped her coffee, listened, and said next to nothing. In her disappointment, she had forgotten to ask if the garage had been cleaned out. But she would find out soon enough. She was here now.

She pulled the truck to a stop in front of the house and reached for her knapsack of essentials. A six-pack of beer, a carton of orange juice, four glasses, protein bars, three packs of smokes, and a four-pack of toilet paper—items to relieve moving stress and aid in the calling of Mother Nature. She doubted the Sebastians had provided toilet paper. Landlords rarely did.

She handed Hillary a plastic bag of frozen foods and juices. "Hill, can you take these into the house? They need to go in the freezer."

"Sure, Mom."

They went inside. The front door opened into a large living room. There was a small mudroom and to the right, a stairwell led up to three bedrooms and a four-piece bathroom. A long hallway led into a separate dining room and the spacious but original kitchen was off to the left. Straight in front of the dining room, another hallway led to a large room that served as a flex-room. It was equipped with a washer and dryer, an open area with plenty of windows that could be used as an office, and a four-piece bathroom. With about 1,550 square feet on two levels, an unfinished basement that would likely serve as a catch-all for all the family's junk, the home was plenty big enough for a family of four—five, if you counted Barney, who would arrive any minute.

Hillary opened the freezer and put the frozen goods inside. Dana pulled out the six-pack and orange juice and put them in the fridge. She cracked a beer as her daughter watched.

"Do you want some juice?"

"Yeah, I'm thirsty."

Dana filled a glass for Hillary, who stood smiling, her soulful brown eyes filling her mother with pride. *She could have turned out a lot worse, given the instability she's lived with.*

"So what do you think, Hill?"

Hillary slurped the juice, draining half the glass in two long gulps. She wiped the orange film from around her lips and pushed back a curly lock of brown hair that had fallen over her eyes. "I like it. I'm going to look around."

"Where are you going?"

"I want to see my bedroom. And then I want to see the pond."

Dana was tired and wanted to see the garage first thing. Besides, there was a lot of unpacking yet to do. "Yours is the first one on the right when you go upstairs. I'll be outside, honey."

She disappeared as Dana fished into the knapsack, lit a smoke and went outside, smoke in one hand, beer in the other.

She frowned as she opened the garage door. It was still packed to the rafters with junk. *Shit. That sucks.* Jackson was supposed to start building cabinets tomorrow, and Dana had a biker client who was supposed to be dropping off a Harley Davidson for a custom mural paint job.

She fished into her pocket for her cell phone and, at the last minute, changed her mind. She would call Seth tomorrow. She was too mentally and physically drained from the move to deal with it right now. She just wanted to get the bare essentials into the house to be able to sleep comfortably for the night, kick back and relax, for a change.

Hillary sprinted off the porch. "I like my room, Mom. I'm going to check out the pond."

Dana produced a fake smile as she recognized the sound of an engine. Jackson had arrived, Barney and Brittany in tow. He pulled to a stop behind the pick-up and opened the door. Barney was the first to come bounding out. He ran up to Dana, skidded to a stop in front of her, examining her closely with his big brown eyes, large pink tongue dangling. He seemed to be reading her expression. She produced another fake smile, patted Barney and kissed him on the top of the head. He barked and bounded off toward the pond.

Brittany smiled at Dana, grabbed two large grocery bags, and disappeared into the house.

Jackson pulled a cooler from the truck—he came prepared—set it on the lawn, extracted a beer and grinned at Dana, his long brown hair tied back in a pony-tail. He popped the top and took a swig.

"What's up, honey?"

"The garage—it's full of shit. How're we supposed to work tomorrow?"

"Did you call the landlord?"

"No. I don't know if I want to deal with them today, Jackson. I'm tired, stressed, and we still have all this shit to unpack and move."

"Do you want me to call?"

"Do you want to?"

"I don't know. I'm sure the landlord's got his shit, like everyone else. But I'm not sure I want to listen to it right now."

"What the hell does that mean?"

"I don't know."

Dana wasn't sure how the observation made sense. But, by some twisted logic, it seemed to. They both laughed, hardly understanding what they were laughing at. Maybe it was the heat. They clinked beer cans, took their respective swills, and kissed.

"Let's get this shit done so we can relax," he said, wiping a sweaty brow.

"What about your friends?" Two of his friends had offered to help with the move in exchange for beer and KFC.

"No shows."

"Why?"

"Eric said it's too far to drive and Randy ... well, he's randy; wants to spend the night screwing his girlfriend."

Dana couldn't help smiling. "Some friends."

"No one likes moving," he said.

"Yeah, but they promised."

"Empty words."

"That's it. Let's get going. It's only us now, anyway," Dana said. She was about to call Hillary in from the pond when she remembered the U-Haul. "What time does that have to be back tomorrow?"

"Not until one in the afternoon."

"Where are we going to put all that shit? It's all work stuff, tools and that."

"We'll call the landlord tomorrow. If they can't get the stuff out right away ... I guess we just put it outside under tarps until we have the garage empty."

"That's fucked up."

"You said you didn't want to call the landlord."

"I changed my mind." In the confusion and stress of the move, Dana had forgotten that they had all their work equipment in a rented vehicle that had to be returned tomorrow. If the garage wasn't cleared out, they would be moving the stuff twice—once onto the lawn under tarps, and eventually into the garage. She hadn't even begun to unpack, and she was already sick of moving. If she didn't have to, she didn't want to move the heavy tools and equipment twice. Not to mention that items sitting on the lawn under tarps would be wide-open targets for thieves. Who knew what kind of riff-raff circulated this area? She had no idea. But she wasn't prepared to take any chances with their livelihood.

She pulled out her cell and called Seth. After four rings, it went to voicemail and she left a message. Satisfied the message was diplomatic enough—not that she ever considered herself a model of diplomacy—she closed the phone and went to work unpacking.

Why wasn't anything easy anymore? Life was such a struggle all the time; pulling tooth and nail for every single thing she wanted. And all she wanted really, thinking about it as she carried box after box into the house, was a roof over her head, a harmonious relationship, the ability to earn a living, and the best for her family. Oh, and maybe a little peace and quiet once in a while, thank you very much.

First Seth wanted her to paint the stairs and stairwell for nothing. Instead of asking, he just *wanted*. A line from a movie, and she couldn't remember what movie, crept into her head.

You've been weighed ... you've been measured ... and you've been found wanting. She didn't think the meaning was quite the same. Did it still fit?

Seth was certainly wanting. He was fucking with her livelihood, her ability to feed, clothe, and house her family.

Wait until tomorrow. He would get a piece of her mind.

Chapter Nine

"Don't give him a piece of your mind," Jackson said the following afternoon as they stood in front of the house, watching a 2010 blue Intrepid barrel down the gravel driveway and narrowly miss Barney. Barney squealed, leaped away from danger, darted up on the front porch and stood guarding the front door, eyeing the intruder cautiously.

"What are you talking about?" Dana bristled. "They almost killed our dog."

"Honey, we want the shit moved as soon as possible. Do you want to start that request with a confrontation?"

The car stopped and Gertrude got out with a smile. "You called?"

Dana bit her tongue as Jackson took over. "Hi ... I thought we were dealing with Seth?"

"Today you're dealing with me."

"Oh."

Dana disappeared into the house. She knew herself well enough to know that if she remained outside, things were going to get a lot worse before they got better—if they got better. They had packed away the essentials last night, finished off only a few beers, and it had been all they could do to crawl into bed and crash. They still had a full day of arranging furniture and unpacking ahead of them, and she wasn't looking forward to it. Who would?

Gertrude addressed Jackson: "What can I do for you?"

"We need the garage," Jackson said.

"Garage?" Her tone suggested she hadn't the foggiest notion of what Jackson was talking about.

"Yeah. There's a whole bunch of stuff still in there still. You guys said you'd get rid of it before we moved in."

"Let's look at it," she said, walking across the lawn.

They opened the door and looked in. Jackson could see for the first time the roof was still leaking. He frowned. Even if the stuff was removed right away, a repair would be necessary.

"Oh, *that* stuff."

By that time, Dana had returned outside and stood on the porch, watching, wondering if she should go to the garage. For now, she vetoed the idea and remained where she was.

"Are you planning on moving it?" Jackson asked.

"I'll have my son come by tomorrow with a pick-up truck and get rid of it."

"You sure?"

"Of course."

"Because I don't want to be hard to get along with or anything ... we're really good people and we don't cause any problems or anything like that." He came closer. "Look into these eyes. Do these look like honest eyes? Does this face look honest? We're good people and all that. We just need that stuff moved." He pointed to the U-Haul. "All our tools are in there and we need to get that back today. Where are we going to put all that stuff?"

"My son will empty the garage tomorrow," she said.

"Yeah, but where does the stuff go today? I got to take it out of the U-Haul. Where am I going to put it?"

"I can have Seth bring you some plastic tarps for now, if you want."

"Okay, okay, that'll have to do."

She began walking back to the car. "I have a present for you."

By this time, Dana had stepped off the porch and was standing on the lawn.

Gertrude reached the Intrepid, popped the trunk, removed five gallons of paint and set them on the grass. "Here's the paint. These three are for the walls ... these two, brown ones, for the stairs." She reached back into the trunk. "Here's some sandpaper. The stairs will need sanding."

Dana's jaw dropped. She bit her tongue.

"Oh, don't you have two vehicles?" Gertrude asked.

"Yeah," Dana said. "One's behind the house."

"I don't want you parking behind the house."

"But the driveway goes all the way around the house."

"No, we need to see your vehicles."

"See our vehicles? For what?" Dana asked.

Gertrude paused for a moment, her eyes darkening. "That's rule 1," she shouted. "No parking behind the house!" Veins bulged in her forehead.

It took her a few seconds to calm down before her tone softened—but only a little.

"Can you move the other vehicle around the front? Oh ... and let me know when you're finished painting. I would like to inspect it." After a short pause, her expression brightened. "One more thing—welcome to the neighborhood." It was a lightning-fast Jekyll and Hyde transformation.

Startled, Dana was about to open her mouth when Jackson put an arm around her shoulder and gave her a look. She closed her mouth without saying a word—another cup of shut the fuck up. And she hadn't even had her morning coffee.

Gertrude waved, got in the car, and sped down the driveway, not even bothering to stop and look both ways before turning onto Rural Route 14.

"That woman's a fucking psycho," Dana said.

"Don't worry about it," Jackson tried to reassure her.

But Dana was seething. "Don't worry about it? Are you kidding me? She promised to clear that shit out of the garage, and it's still there. Now she wants us to start painting the stairs. Starts yelling at us. Well, tit for tat. I'm not lifting a finger until I see that stuff removed."

Barney had by now left the porch and was bounding playfully around the acreage, oblivious to the drama.

Hillary and Brittany had both stepped out on the porch, wondering what all the drama was about.

"Everything okay, Mom?" Brittany asked. Like any nineteen-year-old, she wanted to have some fun.

"Fine, Brittany. Or it will be, anyway."

"What happened?"

Dana didn't have the stomach to regurgitate everything. "We just need the garage cleaned out, honey, but it'll happen. Don't worry. Are you going to help us today?" She looked at both girls, now standing side-by-side on the porch. They nodded. Jackson had already started removing boxes from the U-Haul. He started toward the house with the first load.

"I had a bad dream last night," Brittany said.

"What happened?" Dana asked.

"I got stabbed to death. As I was dying, I watched a lady take some of my blood and put it in a little cup. But I passed out—died, I guess—before I saw what she did with it."

"That sounds messed up," Dana said. At first, she could think of nothing else to offer. Then, "It's only a nightmare, honey. It's not real."

"I know, Mom. I'm not a kid anymore."

Jackson walked out the door, regarding them curiously. "Could we please have these conversations later? I could use some help here."

Chapter Ten

"They don't seem inclined to help us," Dana said that Saturday afternoon, examining the assortment of tarps on the lawn that constituted their tools and equipment. "Never mind help us, just do what they promised to do."

The two girls were down at the pond playing with Barney.

Jackson stood beside her. "Do you want me to call?"

"I've been calling for the last three days and keep getting voicemail."

"Oh."

The Sebastians had not shown up to remove the garage contents or provide the promised tarps. Luckily, Jackson had a few tarps, and now their gear was neatly wrapped in blue plastic, sitting beside the garage. Without the use of the garage, a wrench had been thrown into their work schedule. Jackson had to postpone the cabinet construction, and the client was none-too-happy, pointing out his kitchen renovation had a tight deadline.

Luckily, Jackson had an interior house painting contract starting next week that would bring in some much-needed cash.

And Dana's gas tank paint job also had to be postponed. Rusty, a member of The Skeletons, an Ontario bike gang, sounded a little gruff on the phone when Dana had called and said the workspace they were planning on using to paint the tank was not yet available. "Well, when will it be available?" the biker had asked in a tone that sounded more demanding than questioning. Dana had assured Rusty, an ape of a man, that by the weekend they would get it sorted out. "I'm dropping it off Sunday, then," he had said, leaving no room for argument.

Today was Saturday. Dana knew if she could do a good job with his Harley, there would be more work coming from the other bikers. She wanted to get it done, knowing it could spiral her airbrushing career quickly upwards. She didn't care what the bike gang did for extra-curricular activities. Money was money. Business was business. A few years ago, she had done a wall mural for Rusty, and that had led to two other wall murals. They had paid her in full after completion of the work, even throwing in a generous tip for completing it under the specified time frame. So, there was no problem with payment. She just needed to deliver on time. And so far, she hadn't been able to do that.

Her brow furrowed as she thought about what it would mean to her income if Rusty blew her off. The whole biker contingent would follow suit in an instant, and that well would run dry. Well, she wasn't prepared to let that happen.

"Let's get this shit out of here now," she said.

Jackson didn't argue. "I'll go inside and get some spare boxes."

They had gone a long way to making their house look like a home. Other than the garage issue, the kids and dog were starting to settle in. Inside, most of the boxes had been unpacked, although there was still more work to do.

Dana went to work in the garage, removing tarps, and brought some stuff outside on the lawn, where Jackson began packing it carefully in boxes. There was a lot of junk in the mix: empty tin cans, small, broken appliances, damaged kids toys, some old rusty tools, a couple of rancid and soggy mattresses—even some used syringes. Jackson threw the mattresses to the side and packed away the remaining items.

Three hours later, they had cleared out the contents and were halfway to assembling their tools and equipment inside.

They were both inside the garage when they heard the roar of the engine. Dana peered out a window and saw it—a gray pick-up truck barreling down the gravel driveway at high speed, a cloud of dust billowing up and trailing behind it.

The pick-up sped toward the garage and slammed on the brakes, the tires skidding on the gravel for about ten feet before coming to a stop. A thick cloud of dust wafted into the garage, and Jackson and Dana coughed as a man exited the vehicle.

Gord Sebastian in the flesh, but certainly not at his most diplomatic.

His eyes narrowed. He waved his fists as he stormed inside the garage. He adjusted his Molson Canadian baseball cap, spotted the two, and the vociferous litany began.

"What the hell do you guys think you're doing?" he demanded. "You have no fucking authority to take this shit out of here." He waved at the tarps outside the garage. "All this stuff needs to be put back inside. And get your fucking shit outta' here."

The dust was beginning to settle and Dana could just make out the veins bulging in his neck, one pulsating down the middle of his forehead. His face was red. Dana felt her face beginning to flush as well.

Jackson noticed it and took over. "Who are you, anyway?" It seemed to catch Gord by surprise. He paused for a moment. "My parents own this house. I'm the caretaker."

"We were told the garage comes with the rental," Jackson said, speaking in a calm voice. He was smart enough to realize butting heads with the hothead standing in front of him would not bring about the desired outcome. "And we've been calling Seth for the last three or four days to get this shit out. He didn't answer our calls. He said he'd have you take it out, and we need this space to run our businesses. It's all packed away nice and carefully. We thought we were doing you a favor. Now all you have to do is load it and take it."

Gord wasn't having any of it. "The garage doesn't come with the house. Never did. You guys need to get your shit out of here now and put the other shit back in here." He moved a few feet closer to Jackson and stared him down, evaluating how much of a threat he would be. He thought he could take him.

Dana exploded. "Well, you're fucking wrong, buddy. This was not the deal. We wouldn't have moved here if we had known it wasn't included."

"I said get your shit out of here now," Gord insisted, moving a few inches closer to Jackson, who was not backing down.

"There is no way we're taking our stuff to sit outside and get ruined. That's our livelihood," Jackson said, returning the stare-down with equal menace.

"I'm calling Seth," Dana said. "Better still, I'll drive right to his house and tell him to straighten your ass out. We didn't sign a lease with you. You're not our landlord. Seth and Gertrude are. You can't come barreling down this driveway and harass us like this. I have two kids and a dog. You could have killed someone."

The pulsating vein on Gord's forehead grew larger, his knuckles now white with the force of the fist-clenching. But he glared and said nothing.

Dana wasn't going to wait around thinking about it. It seemed she was getting the upper hand. "You can't come on this property without twenty-four hour written notice. In fact, you can't come on this property at all. We didn't sign a lease with you. And we sure as hell didn't sign up for this harassment."

"I want this stuff taken out," Gord said. But his voice had lost its threatening edge.

"Fuck you," Dana said. "Get the fuck off our property."

"It's my property."

"I don't think so. Not while we're renting it, it isn't. Get the fuck outta' here and don't ever come back."

Gord backed away a few feet, regarding Dana wearily. "I'll come here whenever I feel like it. Rule 2 is, you can't use the garage."

"Oh yeah, try it and I'll call the cops on you." She noticed something in his eyes that she hadn't seen in the earlier angry storm he had blown in with. She thought it was a hint of fear. He was afraid of the law.

But this argument was becoming circular. Soon she would be back to square one. She was about to start yelling, but at the last second she recognized she might lose control of this situation. She took a few deep breaths, backed out of the garage, and retreated to the house.

She heard the animated voices of Jackson and Gord slowly fade out as she stepped up on the porch, lit a smoke, and took a long drag. Then she opened the door and went inside. With an unsteady hand, she reached inside the fridge, grabbed a beer, opened it and took a long pull. It was shortly after noon, but it must be six in the evening somewhere in the world.

She walked to the front door, heard the rumble of an engine, and saw a truck exiting the property, trailed by a billowing cloud of dust.

This was not unfolding the way she had hoped.

Chapter Eleven

Dana had hoped—even prayed—for a solution, and a partial resolution had come. That following Sunday after Gord had left—in his place, but in a huff—Jackson had driven over to the Sebastian residence, a short five-minute drive from the rental, and pleaded with Seth to do two things—keep Gord away from them, and remove the items from the lawn beside the garage. He wasn't yet prepared to enforce the twenty-four hour rule. One thing at a time, or in this case two things at a time. A few hours later, Seth had a utility trailer dropped off beside the garage and indicated he would slowly but surely get around to loading and removing the junk.

A week later, the items remained beside the utility trailer.

But Jackson and Dana had at least begun to work in the garage. Rusty had dropped of his Harley that Sunday just as Seth was leaving the property after dropping off the trailer. Jackson had begun work on the kitchen cabinets, and Dana had created a masterpiece of a gas tank mural—a skull, crossbones, and a nude woman with flowing blonde hair, posing seductively. All on a jet-black gas tank, power-polished and gleaming with two coats of acrylic-urethane clear-coat.

When he picked up the bike on Wednesday, Rusty was suitably impressed. He scratched his grizzled red beard, wiped a hand through his mop of wild red hair, and declared, "This is genius."

He had given her a generous tip and told her more work would be forthcoming. He even agreed to let her photograph the image and post it on Facebook to begin advertising her work. As he was about to pull away, he stopped and studied her momentarily, concern etched in his grizzled face. He had received an edited version of some of the problems they were having with the landlords. "If you ever need any help with these people, you call me. The Skeletons are known for fixing problems."

Dana had given it some serious consideration. But, at least for now, the situation did not warrant biker interference. She had an idea of what kind of tactics Rusty would implement. She knew they would be less than diplomatic. She hoped she wouldn't have to go there. But other disturbing incidents made her wonder.

Seth had driven onto the property at least twice without notice, assuring Dana and Jackson that eventually the items would be loaded into the trailer and removed. He was just "too busy right now." He had also assured her that he had reeled in his son and apologized for Gord's erratic, aggressive behavior, although he said nothing of his wife's temper tantrums.

Gertrude's visits were less welcome. Initially, she had said she wanted to inspect the stairwell painting that Jackson had started on. But, during her unannounced visits, she had implemented two new rules to the growing list. Rule 3, as it were, stipulated verbally that no items were to be stored in the unfinished basement. The reason, according to Gertrude, was that "sometimes the basement leaks a little during heavy rains, and I don't want to be responsible for your stuff getting damaged."

Dana thought about protesting Rule 3, but Jackson gave her that look. So she had only nodded.

On yet another visit, ostensibly to inspect the painting on the stairwell, which she said looked fine, she had implemented Rule 4. "I don't want you inviting a bunch of people here to sleep over. This property is for you and your family, not guests."

Dana had been less willing to acquiesce to Jackson's look with that rule. "It doesn't say anything in the lease about that," she pointed out.

To which Gertrude had launched into an angry and vitriolic temper tantrum, shouting, among other things, "Our rules have to be obeyed, unless you want to end up kicked out on your ass."

Dana was about to open her mouth when her daughters walked in. Hillary noticed the distressed expression on Dana's flushed face and had asked: "Is everything all right, Mom?"

Dana forced a smile and nodded. She was trying to keep her kids out of the war; she wanted at least a semblance of normality and stability for them. But she had no intention of honoring Rule 4.

She also wanted, at least for the time being, to forget everything. She was still a little troubled by the items sitting beside the garage, basically giving the Sebastians free rein to come and go as they pleased. But she didn't want to think about it right now. The move had taken its toll on the entire family and they had little, if any, time to relax.

She sat in silence beside Jackson in a plastic lawn chair on the front porch. They drank cold orange juice, which only provided a modicum of cooling given the intense heat on that Saturday afternoon. With the humidity, the mercury was expected to rise to one hundred and ten degrees Fahrenheit. And, although it was just a few minutes past one in the afternoon, she could already feel the heat's suffocating grip. Her body was sticky with sweat.

On an impulse, she asked, "What're Marty and Sue up to?" Marty and Sue Haginstaff were long-time friends of Dana and Jackson. Marty worked as a backyard mechanic in a garage at the back of a house he rented in Brantford, and Sue was a home-care aid working with seniors. They were both pleasantly plump and fun to hang around.

Jackson wiped his sweaty brow. "Let's invite them over for drinks."

"Why not?" Dana said. "Let's have some fun for a change."

"Yeah, didn't they say they were taking some time off work around now?"

"I did see something on Facebook about it," Dana said.

"Why don't you invite them over? It's a beautiful day. I bet they'd love to get out of the city."

Dana thought about it. The internet and phone were functioning, they had groceries, and most of the household stuff had been packed away. The house still looked a little disheveled, but certainly livable. Besides, she had been under a lot of stress these past few days, and on a few occasions, had to fight to control an outburst. *Problems were like a ball*, she thought. *If you give the ball to someone else, at least for the time being, then they have the problem. Fine, I'll give the ball to the fuck-up Sebastians and get drunk. Or at least have a couple. It could go a long way to relieving some stress.*

"Sure," she said, fishing out her cell phone and speed-dialing. Marty answered and said his air conditioning had just broken down. He could use a trip to the country, if for nothing else than to sit beside a sprinkler and drink beer.

Or maybe they could go swimming in the pond? Dana gave directions and hung up.

An hour later, Marty, Sue, Jackson and Dana sat around the pond on plastic lawn chairs, every once in a while enjoying a refreshing dip. A large cooler of alcoholic beverages kept them company. Barney, Hillary and Brittany had retreated to the comfort of the house, where a few strategically-placed fans and a portable air conditioner provided cool comfort from the heat. The girls were probably posting stuff on Facebook. It's what they did.

"Nice place you have here," Marty said, emerging from the pond. The water dripped down his formidable bulk as he grabbed a towel and wiped his pudgy face. He dried his short blonde hair with a few efficient sweeps, picked up his beer, and settled into a lawn chair.

Dana had already explained the situation with the garage and her creepy feeling about the landlords, and she didn't want to say more—she didn't want to spoil an otherwise fun afternoon. "I hope we can settle in and be happy. It's nice to finally get a break from all the stress of moving."

"A toast to your happiness," Marty said, raising his beer. "You guys will be like The Waltons."

Dana smiled and they clinked cans.

"I hope you're happy here," Sue said, pulling her mid-length brown hair away from her eyes as she took a seat. She snapped a few pictures with her camera.

"I hope so," Jackson said, producing a toothy grin and guffawing with laughter.

They all laughed. Not at what he said, but at his laugh.

"Hey, don't be posting any of those on Facebook," Jackson warned.

"Why not?" Sue asked.

"You should get permission before you do that," he said, getting up and dunking his head in the pond before taking a seat.

"Permission? It's just some photos of us having fun," Sue said. She was an avid Facebooker, posting as often as twelve times a day. Dana was right behind her, a close second. They posted everything and anything. Discretion and good judgment were not part of the equation. Jackson had a Facebook account, but posted very little, and always thought carefully before posting anything.

Marty was adamantly anti-Facebook. He had no account and didn't believe in the social media website, even though it had over a billion users.

"You might think that," Jackson said. "But what if one of my customers sees that and thinks I'm nothing but a party animal? He could fire me, or not hire me, in the case of a potential customer."

"I don't think people would look at that," Sue said unconvincingly.

"I wouldn't be so sure," Marty said. "What about that Vancouver politician, running for some government office. I can't remember his name now. But apparently he was doing well in the polls until the opposition party dug up some Facebook photos of him, much younger and probably a completely different person, dancing with some woman with his hand squarely on one of her breasts. They found another photo of him stripped down to his underwear, holding them open, a few people staring at his ... package."

"I heard the story," Jackson said. "He had to resign. The photos were considered politically inappropriate for someone running for office."

"Exactly," Marty said.

"Yeah, well what about the Hildebrants?" Dana said.

"Hildebrants?" Jackson and Marty said, almost in unison.

Sue picked up the story: "Some woman named Kelly Hildebrant was opening her account one day and it went to another Kelly Hildebrant, a man with exactly the same name. Anyway she messaged him and it eventually led to a marriage. He was the man of her dreams. They have a ton in common and are happily married now. They wouldn't have met if it weren't for Facebook."

"All I'm saying is for every good story about Facebook there's a bad one," Marty said. "Do you know it's the biggest hotbed for computer crime than any other website in history?"

Dana and Sue shook their heads.

"What about business promotion, family and friends?" Dana asked. "It's probably the most powerful marketing tool in the world for promoting a business. And you can do a lot of it for free."

"My point," Jackson said, "is just be careful what you post on there. If it's incriminating, it can and will be used against you."

"All the personal information that people put on ... it's a virtual treasure trove for criminals. If you want something to remain personal, you don't put it on Facebook. Because once it's out there, you can never take it back," Marty said.

"I don't think my friends would do anything like that to me," Dana said.

"Really?" Jackson said. "You have three hundred and something friends on Facebook. How many of them do you actually consider friends?"

Dana didn't respond.

"Half of them, if you're lucky," Marty chimed in. "You know, someone once did an experiment with Facebook. They created an account with a picture of a frog as an alias, sent out—I can't remember exactly—I think it was four hundred friend requests. Do you know how many of them they got back?"

"Half," Jackson guessed.

"Almost half," Marty said. "Half of the people who didn't even know the little frog were prepared to share all their personal information with him."

There was a short silence as everyone digested the information.

Maybe I should consider cancelling my account, Dana thought. She remembered all the times she had drunk-Facebooked, the absolute worst thing to do. And, in the last week, she had posted more than a few derogatory comments about her "landlords from hell."

"All I'm saying," Marty said, "is if you want to keep something personal, you can't trust Facebook to keep it private for you, regardless of how you tweak the privacy settings. Their business model is to sell that information, not to keep it personal. Do you think they do this for fun? It's a business."

"Think about it," Jackson said. "With Facebook, you and all your personal details, likes and dislikes, hobbies, whatever, are exactly what Facebook wants to sell to advertisers. You are the product they're selling." And then, realizing he also had an account, he added: "We are the product."

"What about the benefits of keeping in touch with family ..." Sue was interrupted by the sudden rumble of an engine. The Facebook debate would have to wait for another day.

Dana grimaced and jerked, an involuntary response—maybe a Pavlovian response—to the sound of Gord's pick-up truck speeding down the driveway, a billowing cloud of gray dust trailing his untimely and unwelcome arrival.

"Ahhh, fuck," she said. "What the fuck is he doing here?"

"Who?" Sue asked, alarmed.

"It's the psycho-landlord's psycho son."

Sue craned her neck to see the pick-up truck skidding to a stop on the driveway, about three hundred feet up the gently sloping hill.

"Could you go see what that asshole wants?" Dana asked Jackson.

"I'll join you," Marty said.

They put down their beers and hurriedly walked up the lawn to the driveway, where Gord was parked. By this time, Hillary and Brittany had emerged on the porch and were watching the drama unfold. Barney sat beside them.

Gord strode purposefully down the lawn, yelling and screaming, his fists balled and face rapidly transforming into red—red rage. Until he got close, his rants were unintelligible.

Then Jackson could decipher the words, loud and clear.

"Get the fuck out of the pond," he shouted. "You have no right going in there. Get out now!"

He was close enough now that Jackson could see his eyes. The pupils were dilated. He might be high on crack-cocaine, crystal meth maybe.

"Seth told us we could use the pond ... and so did Gertrude."

It didn't slow him down. He came face-to-face with Jackson, even pushed him back. Jackson stood his ground as Gord continued the rant. "You guys are stealing fish from the pond. I just know it. If I find out who took the fish, I'll cut their fucking heads off!"

Gord cast Marty a menacing stare. "I'll fucking shoot you and your truck!"

Marty had heard enough. He continued up to his vehicle, a red pick-up truck, and extracted a small baseball bat, known as a billy-club in these parts. As Gord and Jackson argued, he slowly approached Gord from behind.

Dana and Sue approached as the heated argument gathered steam.

"Get the fuck out of my house right now," Gord shouted. "You fucking bastards don't obey the rules. Rule 5 is you're not allowed to use the pond!"

Dana knew the girls had actually fished in the pond last week. Brittany had caught two small rainbow trout but had released them back in the water. As far as she knew, none of the girls had kept any of the fish. Maybe Barney had caught a few fish and eaten them? It was possible. But was Gord counting the fish, or scouring the property, looking for fish bones? Dana had no idea, but, as she saw Marty standing behind Gord now, cocking the bat and preparing to deliver a hard blow to the back of his head—maybe the only action that would get through to the imbecile—she snapped.

By now, Gord was pushing Jackson's chest repeatedly, trying to goad him into fighting.

"Get the fuck off our property right now or I'll call the police," she said, while Sue turned the audio-recorder on her smartphone on and began recording events.

Gord dropped his hands and stared. Of the entire group, he seemed frightened of Dana. Like the garage incident, when she started yelling, he listened. Who knew what psychological scarring he might have that was related to women? Dana didn't care. But she did know that if he didn't listen to her soon, she was quite prepared to attack. She was in full adrenaline, self-preservation mode right now and the thoughts that accompanied that power-boost weren't often rational.

"Stay the fuck away from the pond," he shouted. "That's not in the lease."

Marty concealed the bat behind his back as Gord swung around and slowly registered that he was outnumbered. He had come to within seconds of having his skull bashed in.

Dana waved her cell phone at him. "Leave or I'll call the police. And don't ever come back here again."

Sue held up a smartphone. "I'm recording everything you say. Do you have any more death threats?"

Gord stopped talking and slowly eyed the faces watching him. There was a stand-off for a few seconds as he stared at them and they stared back. Finally some dim recognition of reality seemed to enter his mind.

He turned and stormed back to the truck, his hands swinging at his sides like a marching soldier. They watched his body grow smaller as he reached it. He opened the door and, before getting in, stopped.

"Rule 5. Stay the fuck away from the pond. Or else!"

Chapter Twelve

"What else are we supposed to do?" Jackson asked as he drove down the highway in Dana's pick-up truck late morning a few days later. "I mean, these people aren't playing with a full deck, so how do we try and second-guess what they might do? They don't process information normally."

"I guess you're right," Dana said, sucking on a cigarette.

They were discussing their trip to the Brantford detachment of the Ontario Provincial Police. They had reluctantly decided to inform the police of Gord's death threats. Dana had initially resisted going to the police. In her experience, they didn't seem to give a shit, or had more important matters to deal with. But wasn't this an important matter? Gord had threatened to kill them. After the recent rage-filled explosion, Marty and Sue had quickly departed, no longer wanting anything to do with a leisurely day at the pond. It had been ruined.

And, initially, Dana had done nothing, hoping the whole thing would blow over and that Seth and Gertrude could reel their son in. But it hadn't worked. He had returned, angrier than ever. And what worried Dana most was that if they did nothing, and he exploded again, perhaps on another innocent, unsuspecting victim, how could she live with herself if she knew about his instability and did nothing? Worse still, what if he decided to target her family or friends, Marty and Sue in particular?

She had also thought about contacting Rusty. After all, he had offered to "deal with" the situation. But, in the end, she had decided that any action by Rusty or his gang affiliates would lead right back to her. And the result would only escalate the violence, ratchet it up a few notches from its already dangerous level. And she didn't want that.

What had forced her hand was a call from Sue this morning, telling Dana that she and Marty had thought it over and had decided to report the incident to police. She was afraid for her life, and the lives of her husband and two teenage daughters. She was not prepared to let the whole thing blow over.

She wanted to press charges.

So she and Marty had gone into the station that morning, reported the incident, and given their statements to Constable Lorenzo Sealing, the cop who had earlier told Dana and Jackson, "I'm not your babysitter, you know."

Now Dana and Jackson were headed to the detachment to give their statements. Afterward, she was told, the cop planned on arresting Gord. Perhaps unwittingly, Constable Sealing had become their babysitter. Karma. You couldn't avoid it.

They pulled into the parking lot, found an empty stall, parked, and entered the station. A middle-aged, stressed-out policewoman told them to have a seat momentarily. Sealing would be right with them.

A few minutes later, he entered the lobby, his eyes a little tentative, perhaps showing a small sign of embarrassment. They would never know. He sat down beside them. Introductions were made.

"Thanks for coming in," Sealing said.

They nodded.

Slowly a flicker of recognition swept across his clean-cut face. It flushed not quite red, but a pale pink. He quickly composed himself. "Uh ... we met the other day, didn't we?"

They nodded. Dana shifted uncomfortably on the wooden bench.

"Uh ... sorry about that. I was ... my mind was somewhere else. I was busy with another case."

"I could imagine," Dana said, wanting to move on to the reason they were there.

"What I want to do is bring you both down the hall, put you in separate rooms. I'll take one statement, and my partner, Rod Sebring, will take the other."

"Let's get it over with," Dana said. "Does he have a history with you guys?"

There was a moment's pause as the cop decided how to answer. There were privacy issues. "He's had contact with our department before, but I'm not at liberty to discuss what, if any, charges he might have faced."

Sealing wondered if the recent complaint from the young lovebirds who had been threatened with a gun while making out on Rural Route 14 had anything to do with Gord Sebastian. After all, he lived close to where the couple had claimed the assault had occurred.

"I thought so," Dana said as she followed Sealing down the hall. Jackson disappeared into another room with Sebring. "I thought he had a criminal history."

An hour later, after giving her statement, she stood outside in the hall, talking to Sealing. Jackson had finished and was waiting in the lobby.

"I'm going to arrest him today," Sealing said. "He'll be charged with uttering death threats, taken in, and booked. We won't be able to hold him, though. He'll be released right away."

"What's the maximum penalty for that?" Dana asked.

"Five years, but I doubt he'll get that much ... even if we win."

"Can you keep him away from us?"

"I'm going to talk to his parents, order him not to go near the property, but I can't guarantee he'll comply."

"Another thing," Sealing said. "I want you to keep documenting everything that happens with the landlords and their son. It'll help our case, especially if they continue to harass you."

"I will," Dana said, wondering what the future would hold. She was starting to become scared for her life and her family, living in the so-called paradise.

"I would also start looking for another home. When the parents find out Gord is facing a serious charge, I don't imagine they'll be all that cooperative." He handed her a card. "Call me directly if you feel you're being threatened. There are two more numbers on there if I'm not available."

A few minutes later, Dana felt somewhat relieved as she fired up her truck, glanced at a nervous Jackson anxiously lighting a cigarette, and started the journey home. She knew they had to leave the rental.

But where were they going to go?

Chapter Thirteen

"Where are we going to go?" she asked Sue over the phone about an hour later.

"Find another apartment?" Sue said.

"Yeah, but how? The rental market is tight around Brantford. Most places cost about $1,300 a month. We can't afford that. Besides, we don't have any money." She felt the weight of financial stress settle over her along with a wave of despair. She doubted any of her three hundred plus Facebook friends would help. Come to think of it, only about ten of them were actually real friends, and she knew their financial situation was limited. She also knew Sue and Marty were struggling to raise their kids. Like she, they lived from paycheck to paycheck, hand to mouth.

Dana doubted her siblings—two brothers and two sisters—were in any financial position to help. Even if they were, she was too proud to ask. Her mother was living in subsidized housing, so that was out of the question. She had a couple of rich uncles, but they were heavy into religion, and had long ago decided that Dana and her older brother Jake were black sheep of the family and, not only were they not worthy of a loan, they were not worthy, period. The uncles, along with most of the relatives from her mother's side of the family, had all but disowned them. All very successful, it seemed they had a problem helping out those less fortunate, particularly if it involved family members who didn't toe the line in terms of their faith.

Her uncles had black-and-white versions of religion. In Uncle Henry's eyes, if you weren't of the Christian faith, then you were evil—an extreme Christian fundamentalist view. In his eyes, there was no such thing as agnostic, or spirituality not attached to any form of institutionalized religion, specifically Christianity. In his judgment, along with the judgment of most of his family, shades of gray did not exist.

That well had run dry a long time ago.

"Don't you have anyone who can help you?" Sue asked.

"I've thought all that through. I don't think so."

"You know we're in no position to help you, right?"

"Yeah, Sue. I do."

"So you haven't been able to find anything?"

"My friend Lorena did find us a place. It's cheap, nine hundred a month, but it's in the same shitty complex we just moved from."

"It's still better than living in fear."

"I know, but it's not available until October. I don't think I can wait that long."

"I don't think you should."

"No."

"And my other friend Penny said she knows of someone with a trailer on an acreage who might be able to help us until we find a place."

"That could be good."

"Yeah, but I haven't heard from her in a while. I think she's laying low until all this blows over. You know lots of people don't want to help—they don't want to get involved because they're afraid."

"Can you blame them?"

"I guess not. It'd be like me inviting a bunch of friends out here for a camping weekend after I've been posting a bunch of negative stuff about the landlords on Facebook."

"I don't think anyone would show up."

"I doubt it," Dana said.

"What about a hotel?" Sue asked.

"I've thought of that. I drove by one today with a pool in Brantford. The sign said monthly and weekly rates. A pool would be nice in this heat."

"For sure."

"But with the kids we'd have to rent two rooms, and what about the dog? Who would take Barney?" Dana knew better than to ask Sue. She already had a dog and two cats. There was a very good possibility the animals wouldn't get along. Besides, by indicating the placement of Barney would be a problem, she had surreptitiously asked the question.

"That could be a problem," Sue said. "What about camping?"

"Camping? What about all our shit? We still need to find a home for it. And how do we carry on business from a tent?"

It seemed there was no easy answer. "Whatever you do, you can't stay there," Sue said. "I think if you do, something is bound to happen. And, trust me, it'll be real ugly. You're dealing with a family of psychos."

After a moment's pause, Dana said: "You know I've made a *Beware of Gord* sign that I've been thinking of putting on the lawn."

"I wouldn't. That'll just provoke him."

"I know. Maybe when we're gone."

"Maybe then—but definitely not now," Sue said.

"This isn't over," Dana said. "It's far from over. If Gord goes to jail, Rusty has some friends that'll pay him a visit."

"A friendly visit?"

"Yeah, right. He'll get the shit kicked out of him."

There was the sudden rumble of an engine outside, and Dana abruptly craned her neck. Looking out the living room window, she saw a black pick-up truck parked halfway down the driveway, the engine slowly revving up. Two people were inside.

"I've got to go. There's some shit going down outside."

She hung up and ran outside. The two girls were inside, probably playing on the computer, and Barney was asleep in a corner of the living room. He stirred and raised an eye at her as she flew out the door.

Jackson, who was in the garage building the kitchen cabinets, had stepped out and stood watching the truck, an electric sander in his hand.

Without thinking, Dana ran toward the intruding pick-up. As she got to within twenty feet or so, two men exited, one holding signs and the other holding a sledge hammer. She didn't recognize either of them. And she wasn't in the mood for formal introductions. "What do you guys think you're doing here?" she demanded.

The man holding the signs was tall and gaunt, wearing a grease-stained red baseball cap. Bruce Hammerstein didn't respond to the query. He just stood there, staring blankly while holding the *No Trespassing* signs, an unwilling participant in the escalating battle.

The other man, probably in his early sixties, had a large stomach, the result of too many after-hours junk food snacks.

He had thick, shortly-cropped gray hair and a neatly-trimmed gray beard. "I'm Ben Sebastian," he said. "Seth's brother."

"I don't care who you are," Dana said. "You can't come on this property without giving us notice."

He pulled out two pieces of paper and extended them to Dana, who remained twenty feet away. "One's a map, marking the no trespass zones. The other one's a notice to inspect the property next Sunday between noon and five."

By this time, Jackson, curious to hear the dialogue, was beside Dana. He put an arm around her. "Let me take the papers," he said.

Dana stared at him, her eyes narrowing to slits. Her gaze returned to Ben and Bruce. "What do you want to inspect the property for?"

"We want to see if any repairs are necessary," he said, approaching.

Jackson extended a hand and took the papers.

"What are you doing?" Dana said.

Jackson rolled his eyes and said nothing.

"We're going to put these signs up and be out of your hair," Ben said. "Besides the pond, which is a huge liability for the landlords if you swim in it, there are other areas of the property they do not want you trespassing on."

Dana was about to order them off the property.

"Go ahead and put them up," Jackson said.

Dana bit her lip. She didn't want an argument with her boyfriend right in front of these people. He would get told. But not right now.

A while later, the men had hammered eight *No Trespassing* signs around the property, paying special attention to the pond. They placed four around it, the others marking the boundaries of the acreage.

"Rule 6," Ben said as he put the sledgehammer in the back of the truck and climbed in. "Don't go beyond the signs. Don't trespass."

Dana's face was a deathly-white by the time the truck had peeled out of the driveway and disappeared. She made a point not to say anything to Jackson until the vehicle had vanished.

Still standing in the driveway, wide-eyed, she saw something out of the corner of her eye, parked on the shoulder, close to the entrance. It was Gertrude's car.

Jackson had already started returning to the garage, perhaps aware that to hang around would mean a tongue-lashing. He just wanted to be left alone to complete his work with a semblance of normalcy.

Dana, on the other hand, had seen enough for one day. She ran down the driveway, stopping about twenty feet from the road.

Gertrude stood, arms crossed, staring at her silently.

"Hey, you fucking psycho bitch," Dana shouted. Gertrude's eyes narrowed but she said nothing. "I've got a rule for you. Rule 1: stay off this property unless you give us a damned good reason and a twenty-four hour notice."

Gertrude opened her mouth, but perhaps thought better of engaging in a verbal sparring match. She closed it again.

"You got something to say? Let's hear it!"

And, as ridiculous as it sounded, less than five seconds after telling Gertrude never to set foot on the property without proper notice, Dana abruptly changed her mind and invited her over. "Come here and open your mouth, Gertrude. Right here. Right where I'm standing. I dare you."

Dana clenched her fists and knew one thing for sure. If Gertrude stepped on the property, she would be the recipient of more than a couple hard shots to the head. "Come here, Gertrude. I dare you."

Gertrude didn't budge—only stood and stared.

Dana heard the sound of gravel crunching and looked behind. It was Jackson, coming to rescue her from the outburst.

"Don't engage her," he said, approaching. "What do you think you're doing? You're going down to their level, behaving no better than them."

Dana was about to start shouting at Gertrude again, but for the time being the urge left her. Jackson's voice of reason had prevailed. Slowly she unclenched her fists and felt the anger slowly dissipate. She had to admit, as much as she must have looked like a lunatic running down the driveway shouting at the landlady, it felt good to vent some frustration, even if it was a stupid decision to start calling Gertrude out.

Gertrude opened her car door and stopped. "Rule 7: don't disrespect your landlord." Before Dana could respond, Gertrude got in, slammed the door and drove away.

Jackson put a comforting arm around Dana. She had to hold back an impulse to bid her farewell with the one finger salute. For the first time, she noticed her heart rate—rapidly thumping—as Jackson steadied her. He looked at her with a toothy grin. How could she say anything now about how he didn't take her side earlier? Besides, she wasn't mad anymore. At least for the time being, she was seeing clearly—not through a lens clouded by seething anger and rage.

As they were about to turn and walk back to the house, they heard another vehicle. They spun around and looked. It was a cop car—and sitting in the backseat, glaring at them as it passed, was Gord Sebastian.

His features were knotted with rage.

Chapter Fourteen

"Keep the rage at bay," Gord said out loud a few days later as he drove into Brantford to pick up his fifteen-year-old daughter, Emily. His ex-wife Aaralyn had called earlier in the day to say Emily would be waiting at the hair salon where Aaralyn worked.

With one hand, he squeezed a rubber ball, something his anger management counselor had told him two years ago would help to dissipate the rage that often boiled over inside him. After Aaralyn divorced him, it was a condition of the joint custody that he attend anger management courses and see a counselor. Otherwise, he wouldn't get to see Emily. Considering his behavior, he was lucky to see his daughter at all.

His three-year marriage had been less than harmonious. He had verbally abused Aaralyn, threatened to kill her a few times, and, the proverbial straw that broke the camel's back, flew into a rage one day and beat the shit out of her.

It was out of fear that she hadn't charged him—fear for her life. And there was also money involved. Gord's parents had stepped in with half a million dollars of hush money. So Aaralyn had buttoned her lips, bought a nice house in Brantford, opened a hair salon, and carried on with her life. Money goes a long way in changing a person's moral fiber. But, at least she had pointed out to her lawyer—without coming right out and telling him that she had been physically and verbally abused—that Gord had anger management issues. So, the judge had decided that as a condition of the divorce, Gord attend a course and see a counselor for a year.

That tour of duty was over now, and he no longer needed to comply with any court order. Now he had a far more important court date on the horizon. There would be a preliminary inquiry for his death-threat charge in another two months. So far, Aaralyn hadn't found out about it. But in a city the size of Brantford—just under 100,000—he didn't think it would take long for the word to get out.

The gossip grapevine traveled quicker than the speed of sound.

And Aaralyn, now that she had been paid off, had become increasingly resistant to allowing Gord access to his daughter. She had started using excuses like "She's sick today" or "She wants to sleep over at a friend's," even "She doesn't want to see you this weekend."

Gord thought if Aaralyn found out about the upcoming court case, she would use it against him and apply for complete custody of Emily, one of the few people in Gord's life who actually meant something to him. He wouldn't say he loved her, didn't know what love was, had never experienced it, but he was very fond of her. And he would do anything to ensure Aaralyn didn't find out about the new charge.

He had a few ideas, but now was not the time to think about them. He had arrived at Sassy Styles. As he pulled into the parking lot, he noticed a green four-door sedan backing out of a stall, seemingly oblivious that he was only three feet away. He tossed the ball on the seat and slammed on the brakes, leaning on the horn at the same time, stopping within inches of the vehicle.

He stuck his head out the window. "Hey, why don't you watch where you're going, you stupid fuck?"

An elderly woman with a wavy Marilyn-Monroe-hairstyle rolled her window down and eyed him, frustration etched in her aged features. "I'm sorry. Why don't you mind your manners, young man?" Maybe the sassy style had given her an edge. "Hasn't anyone ever taught you to respect your elders?"

Gord felt the single large vein on his forehead expand and pulse. He opened his mouth to speak—actually, yell. Who did this old bag think she was talking to?

Aaralyn opened the door to the salon and stood there, Emily at her side. "Don't harass my customers."

Gord closed his mouth, grabbed the rubber ball, and began squeezing. He said nothing as he fought to reinstate a normal countenance.

The old woman looked at Gord, then back at Aaralyn. "Do you know him?"

"Unfortunately yes." Aaralyn brushed back her flowing blonde hair, put a hand on her hip and nodded as Emily's eyes darted back and forth between her parents.

"You should teach him some manners," the woman said.

"Say you're sorry," Aaralyn insisted. Her soft blue eyes twinkled and a smile crossed her lips, revealing perfectly aligned pearly white veneers, compliments of the Sebastian family. She was an attractive woman.

Gord squeezed the ball and bit his lip so hard a tiny fountain of blood squirted into his mouth. "I'm very sorry, ma'am. Now could you please continue backing up so I can park?"

By this time, two more cars had pulled in behind and drivers were curiously watching the drama unfold.

"Sorry about that, Ethel," Aaralyn said. "The next haircut is on me."

Ethel paused momentarily and finally smiled at the result of her sass. "Thanks," she said. And, casting Gord a disapproving look along with a waving finger of reprimand, got in her car, backed up, and drove away.

Gord pulled into the now vacant stall and pushed open the passenger door. Emily kissed Aaralyn and got in the truck, bewilderment in her brown eyes.

"Have her back here by six on Sunday," Aaralyn said. "You show up for five seconds and you're already costing me money." She waved to her daughter and disappeared into the salon.

"What's wrong, Dad?" Emily said, searching Gord's eyes. She had wavy brown hair, soft features, and inquisitive eyes.

"Nothing, honey," he said, squeezing the ball and breathing deeply, the pulsating vein in his head slowly shrinking. "What do you want to do this weekend?"

Chapter Fifteen

"It's this weekend," Dana said that Saturday afternoon. She stood in the garage, watching Jackson work. He was applying the last clear-coat of acrylic urethane on the oak cabinets. The roof had been tarped off to keep the area dry and two small fans positioned at windows channeled the toxic fumes from the spray gun outside. The air compressor thumped noisily.

He finished spraying the last cabinet, removed the respirator, set the paint gun down and approached her. A cloud of white mist hung in the air and slowly swirled toward the fans. "Let's go outside. You don't even have a mask. You shouldn't be breathing this shit. It'll kill you."

Dana could think of a few other things that were killing her. She hadn't had a good night's sleep in over a week and felt like a prisoner in her own home. She alternated between feelings of anxiousness and depression.

They closed the door and stood in the hot afternoon sun. Jackson lit a smoke. "What did you say? I couldn't hear you with all that noise."

"It's this weekend."

"What's this weekend?"

"The inspection. It's tomorrow."

He frowned. "Oh, right. So we let them through, and keep looking for another apartment."

"I don't want to let them through."

"Why not?"

"Because they're fucking psychos."

The cumulative effects of lack of sleep were starting to take a toll on Dana. Although the past few days had passed relatively uneventfully, with comparatively less drama, there were still some unnerving events that had transpired. Last night, the same black pick-up truck had pulled into the driveway, driven halfway down, and revved its motor for a few seconds before rumbling away. Dana had leapt off the porch and sprinted after it, wielding a claw hammer. If the truck had stayed, she didn't know what she would have done. She would like to think reason would have prevailed, and she would have simply ordered the vehicle off the property.

But she wasn't sure anymore.

And there was still the drive-by stalking. She had spotted vehicles driving by the property, slowing down, and stopping in front of the house for a few minutes before continuing on.

Gord's gray pick-up was among the stalking vehicles.

She had even called Constable Sealing, but he had said it was perfectly legal for landlords to drive by their property, even stop for a few minutes, as long as it was on a public road. There was nothing he could do.

"Well, if we don't let them in, it's just going to provoke them even more," Jackson said. "I told you, you can't reason with these people. You don't know how they process information."

"I don't care. I don't want them here. I'm not letting them in."

Jackson took a couple of deep breaths. So far, he had been controlling his rage, but now he also felt the cumulative effects of lack of sleep and anxiety, living under the constant threat of attack—a prisoner in his own home. He was tired. "I think it's fucking stupid what you're thinking," he blurted out, immediately regretting it as soon as the words escaped.

Dana's eyes narrowed to slits. "Are you calling me stupid?"

"No, I'm saying your idea is stupid."

"Well, if I have a stupid idea, doesn't that make me stupid?"

There was a moment's pause. He knew that to say the wrong thing at this juncture could escalate the argument into a full scale blow-out. "I didn't say you were stupid. I just don't like the idea."

Dana bristled. There was no turning back. "Well, I think you're stupid too. Acting like nothing's going on ... not taking my side when I try and kick them off the property." Her face flushed red. She opened her mouth to continue the verbal assault, but suddenly felt sick to her stomach. She staggered near the garage and began hacking and puking.

Jackson knew better than to approach her. She was fit to be tied. This was not a battle he could win. He didn't even want to win. He knew it was the situation—the slow building of anxiety—that had brought them both well over the boiling point. So he retreated into the garage, closed the door behind him, and left her retching outside, a milky-white vomit spewing from her mouth with such force it bounced off the grass, tiny droplets soiling her legs and flip-flop sandals.

Part of him felt bad for leaving her like that, but another part told him, under the circumstances, it was for the best. He made up his mind to let her cool down a bit. Then he would apologize.

Fifteen minutes later, some of the color had returned to Dana's features as she walked around the house, checking to make sure all the weapons were where they were supposed to be. They had been living under such fear lately, weapons were hidden around the house, all within easy reach should things suddenly escalate into a fight for survival. Hell, wasn't it a fight for survival already? She thought so as she reached under her mattress, felt the wooden comfort of a hammer handle, and readjusted it. She had already checked Brittany's room, located the baseball bat in the closet and had one more room on the second floor—Hillary's room—before checking the main floor weapons cache. Hillary was busy on the computer and smiled at Dana as she entered.

Dana produced a half smile as she opened the closet door. She located the auto-body mallet and pulled it out. It was time to tell her other daughter. She had already told Brittany that if she was defending her life, she shouldn't hesitate to use the baseball bat.

She produced the mallet.

"What's that for?" Hillary asked.

"If someone comes into your room, you use this on them if you feel threatened." She waved the hammer about three feet from Hillary's face. She probably could have explained it better, but, in her stressed-out state, it was the best she could do. It would have to be good enough.

"Why would anyone want to come into my room?" Hillary asked.

"I don't know, honey. I'm just saying. You understand?"

Hillary nodded. "You don't look so good. Is everything okay?"

Dana nodded unconvincingly.

"Mom, I found something for us."

"What's that?"

"A three-bedroom house in Brantford." She pointed at a Kijiji ad on the computer screen. "It looks really good and it's only a thousand a month."

Dana sat down on the bed as Hillary clicked through the photos. The house showed well, with a lot of renovations.

"Do they allow dogs?" Dana asked.

Hillary clicked on the ad copy. "It doesn't say no dogs."

"Print it out, honey. I'll call them." She said it more to please Hillary than anything else. Unless they could negotiate terms with a landlord, they weren't in a financial position to cough up first and last month's rent and then have to pay all the moving expenses for a new home. They simply didn't have the money. Until they could save enough money to leave, they were, in a very real way, trapped.

Hillary printed the ad and handed it to over. Dana got up to leave. She reached the bedroom door.

"Mom, can Brad come over today?"

Brad was Hillary's boyfriend. She had not been allowed to invite him to the property since they'd moved in. Hillary had only seen him once; when, on a grocery trip into town, Dana had dropped Hillary off at Brad's house for a two-hour visit.

A boyfriend at fourteen. They sure start young nowadays. "I don't think it would be a good idea. I'm not feeling that great today. Maybe next week sometime." Dana had no intention of inviting any more guests over until her problem was solved. Hillary frowned and slowly cast her eyes back to the computer screen. "Can I go see him?"

"Tell you what, I'll take you into town next week to see him."

The frown curled into a half smile. "Thanks, Mom."

Dana went downstairs and checked the rest of the weapon locations. When she was satisfied that everything was in its place, she found the misplaced inspection notice, the new map specifically denoting no-trespass zones, walked out onto the porch, sat down in the shade in a plastic lawn chair, and lit a cigarette.

She studied the map that earlier she had only glanced at. It was hand-drawn in black ink. The no-trespass zones were highlighted with red lines, effectively cutting off the pond and garage. The signs were marked with red X's. Dana was sure the lease specified use of the garage. She would have to double-check. At the top left, the Sebastians had written: *copies to Dana Vilner, Jackson LaPrairie and Brantford, Ontario Provincial Police (OPP).*

What? They gave the OPP a copy. What were they up to, trying to act all legal and everything after they had implemented a slow and methodical torture through intimidation?

What could she do to counteract this tactic? She scratched her head and smoked, trying to think of what they had in mind by notifying the police. Oh, right. They were trying to cover all bases. They knew any further intimidation would not bode well for Gord's upcoming trial, so they were pretending to go by the book. *But what can I do?*

Then it dawned on her. Along with documenting everything, which she had been doing since pressing charges against Gord, she would also file a report with the landlord-tenant board in Brantford. If they won the hearing, perhaps some money would be reimbursed to help them relocate. At the very least, maybe she could help other unfortunate tenants from falling victim to these demented people.

She had been stupid to try to disallow the inspection. She would let it proceed, document everything, and file it with the landlord-tenant board. And she would do it first thing next week.

It made her feel a little better. They still had to live here. She heard a door creaking closed and saw Jackson exit the garage, peel his coveralls off and toss them on a hook. He wore a guilty, apologetic expression.

"I'm sorry," he said as he stepped on the porch.

"So am I." She stood up and they hugged.

The door opened and Brittany peered out. "Am I interrupting something?"

"No," Dana said. "What's up?"

"Can I go into town and visit Shelly? I haven't been out in a long time. I'm getting bored."

That meant Brittany wanted to borrow Dana's truck.

There was a moment's pause. "Okay, but be careful. And if you have any trouble, call me. Make sure you bring your phone. And don't stay out too late."

Brittany nodded. "I'm going to take Barney. He needs a change of scenery too."

Dana didn't object.

When Jackson sat down, Dana asked: "Do you have any friends who could loan you some money?"

She didn't even bother to ask about his family. He was estranged from both parents, low-income alcoholics who eagerly awaited their next pension check so they could buy more booze, get drunk, and become verbally abusive to one another. They seemed to thrive on regular alcohol-induced debates, even knock-down-drag-out fights. And she also knew his older brother Rick was still in jail serving out a drug-trafficking conviction.

Jackson had good reason not to associate with them. He didn't want to be like them.

Jackson thought about it for a moment and shook his head. "Most of my friends are doing worse than me," he said, wondering if he was hanging around with the wrong crowd. At least they were better than the last motley crew whom he had called friends. Most of them were either in jail or conducting their lives in ways that would eventually land them behind bars.

"I didn't think so," Dana said. "But I thought I'd ask anyway."

"Why?"

"Hillary found a house in Brantford that looks pretty good. But I don't even want to call them unless we have enough money." Dana had been fired from her home-care position after sleeping in one too many times. Even though she had told her boss she was having trouble sleeping, and was being harassed by her landlords, the boss had very little sympathy.

She was too stressed-out and mentally fried to do airbrushing even though she knew it was a way out. She had turned down two requests from the bikers for gas tank paint jobs, telling them she was taking some time off.

She knew it was only a matter of time before they found another painter. The only good thing was gang leader Rusty had put in a good word. She suspected, out of loyalty to him, a few of the bikers might wait until she *was* ready to work.

But they wouldn't wait forever. She would have to get her shit together, and soon, if she expected to keep the biker contingent as clients.

"I've got two checks coming," Jackson said. "One next Friday from the cabinets, and the other the Friday after that for the interior painting job."

Two weeks. Dana didn't know if she could last that long. "Well let's start looking now." "I'm going to phone that place in Brantford. Maybe we can stall until you get paid."

Jackson nodded.

"And I'm going to document everything with these psychos and submit it to the landlord-tenant board. We can have a hearing, maybe get our money back."

"Sounds good to me. What about the inspection tomorrow?"

"Let them inspect the property."

Chapter Sixteen

"We're here to inspect the property," Ben said, standing in front of the house the following afternoon, wearing a black t-shirt with a white skull and cross-bones screen-printed on the front. Gertrude stood beside her husband's brother in horn-rimmed sunglasses, arms folded across her yellow blouse. Ben continued: "Depending on how things go, it's going to determine how things roll. And things haven't gone that well lately ..."

"Not on our side ..." Jackson began but was interrupted by Dana.

"You know we don't really want a whole lot of communication anymore, sorry ..."

"I've never destroyed a property or wrecked it or anything like that. I'm not going to do anything like that. I've never been that type of person ever, man," Jackson interrupted.

"If you want to do your property inspection, go right ahead and do that," Dana said, hiding behind a video camera.

"Why can't we talk, Dana? Why's it so hard to talk?" Jackson said.

"It's obviously not gone on a good foot," Ben said. "That's why Gertrude is not talking. Hey, I'm not taking sides here. I've heard one side, and there are always two sides to every story. I'm here to talk about things. We're not here to disrupt anyone's lives. You know we're busy people and everything. That's the last thing we want to do."

"I know," Dana said. "You're very busy."

"We have a couple of proposals. We don't know if it's going to suit. We're just going to air it out, okay," Ben said. "The real issue is the pond. It's a liability for them to have people swimming in it. If something were to happen, then the landlords would be held liable."

"Well, Seth told me I could go in the pond," Jackson said. "In fact, he told me in front of everyone I could go in. But it's not a big deal ... I don't care."

"Why didn't they tell us right of the bat that we couldn't use the pond?" Dana asked, her hand clenching the video camera so tight the knuckles were turning white. "Instead of having Gord barrel down the driveway, threaten to shoot us and cut our fucking heads off for stealing fish. We don't know anything about any missing fish."

Ben ignored the comment. "All I'm saying is that the boundaries as they are specified in the map I gave you the other day show you where you can and cannot go. The police told us if we don't want you on certain areas of the property, technically we should post no trespassing signs and draw a map of the boundaries of the rented premises."

"We don't have a problem with that," Dana said. "But threatening to shoot people is no way to handle it."

"That's a different issue and that will be resolved in the courts," Ben said.

"You think we wanted to go to the police?" Jackson said. "I tried for days to try and resolve things, but couldn't. In the end, our friends forced our hand."

"I'm not going to get into any of that," Ben said. "You guys have decided to take that route. That's fine, you know. Whatever happens—happens."

"You know," Jackson said. "If you were here from the beginning, we would have no issues at all."

"I've got a few rental properties of my own," Ben said.

"That's how it should be," Jackson said, chuckling. "Not tell us one thing and then freak out though."

Dana's face flushed. "I'm sorry, but with you guys there's no reasonable just coming over and saying do you mind not using the pond. It's barreling down. It's calling us liars, threatening to shoot people. That's a slight overreaction."

"That wasn't done by the landlords," Ben said.

"Well, he's acting as their agent. It's the same difference," Dana said.

Ben had no response. Gertrude stood silently while Barney wandered around the large green space playfully, seemingly the only one enjoying the sunny Sunday afternoon.

"I'm going to tell you," Dana said. "We haven't even been here a month. And we have had no enjoyment of the property whatsoever—constantly being visited, constantly being called liars, constantly being harassed and yelled at. These people are paranoid. We feel threatened on this property. We have kids and we don't feel safe here. And the barreling down the driveway, there's no need for that. My dog or my kids could get killed. What we've dealt with here is way beyond what anyone would consider normal."

"I fully understand. I've heard what's happened, and I ..."

"We can't even live here nicely," Dana said, her voice rising. "What is even the purpose of the inspection?"

"The landlords are concerned because they think you're mad at them over what happened—that you may wreck the place."

"Wreck the place?" Jackson said. "I've repaired the garage roof, we painted the steps and stairwell and done other small repairs. The place is better than when we got here."

"We're not people like this," Dana said, her eyes narrowing to slits. "We don't do that kind of thing. I just don't get it. After all that, you're talking about an agreement. What kind of agreement do you want now?"

"They just want to see the house to make sure it hasn't been damaged," Ben said. "We're just trying to break the situation down, because it's been building up and building up. You're distressed, they're distressed. Everybody's distressed."

"No tenant should have to go through this," Dana said.

"Let's let a little air out of the tire here," Ben said, motioning down with open palms. "If you have a problem, maybe I can mediate and you can deal with me instead of them."

"I just want to tell you," Dana said, not letting up an inch. "They have crossed the line so far ..."

"Well, they're inexperienced," Ben said.

"No, they're not. They've had other tenants before. By now they should have enough experience that they don't come threatening to shoot people to solve their problems," Dana said.

"This is not a play matter," Jackson said. "This is not a funny matter."

Gertrude smiled.

"See, she thinks it's funny," Dana said.

Gertrude went and stood by her vehicle, Barney following at her side.

"We're just trying to live," Jackson said. "We just want to live."

"You know what," Dana said. "We'll be quiet right now so you can explain what it is you want to say. If you need to look inside the house go right ahead. We've got nothing to hide."

"It's more that she wants to see inside. After everything that's happened," Ben said.

"They're out of their minds, okay?" Dana said in a calmer tone of voice. "They're out of their minds."

"We never started any of this," Jackson offered. He moved a few feet closer to Ben. "Look at me in my eyes and you'll see I'm a straight-up honest dude, man. I just want to live."

"You haven't liked it, they haven't liked it. I'm trying to bring this situation down."

"I do believe I have a right to state how I feel," Dana said. "This is not normal behavior from landlords. The only thing normal they've done is served us with a proper notice to inspect the property. And you did that."

"I own rental properties," Ben said.

"So you know how it is," Dana said.

"Let's look at the house," Ben said. "If it's in good condition, maybe I can work that in and get them to back off and that way if they've got a problem, they talk to me and if I feel it's worthy enough, I will come and speak to you about it. So, I got to try and ... mediate things, I guess."

"Okay, go ahead then," Dana said.

"I'm not taking anybody's side," Ben said. "I'm trying to be neutral."

"Nobody's upset at you over anything," Dana said. "I'm just upset at the whole situation. If you want to see the house, go ahead."

"She wants to," Ben said.

"Go get her then. Nobody's stopping you," Dana said.

Ben waved Gertrude over. They all went inside the house, Barney leading the tour. Gertrude opened a hallway closet and peered in.

"Would you like to look through our personal items in the drawers as well?" Dana asked.

Gertrude silently continued inspecting the main floor. Seemingly satisfied, she went upstairs, followed by the others. She entered the master bedroom and opened a closet.

"Are you looking at our items or are you looking at things to repair?" Dana asked.

"Dana, just let her look," Jackson said. "You're making it worse."

"I'm just curious," she said, frowning.

Gertrude approached a locked bedroom door and turned the handle.

"My daughter's sleeping in there," Dana said. "You might want to try the other bedroom."

Gertrude kept turning the locked door handle. Dana raised her voice. "Will you please go look in the other bedroom? My daughter is asleep in there."

Gertrude silently went inside the other bedroom. Finding nothing out of the ordinary—the weapons were well hidden—she went downstairs and into the basement, followed by the others. A single incandescent light bulb popped as she flicked the switch. The basement went black.

"Do you have another light bulb?" Ben said.

"No, but I have a flashlight," Jackson said, rummaging around in a kitchen drawer for a few seconds before producing it and handing it to Gertrude. She turned it on, entered the basement, flashlight beam guiding her way. Ben followed. Dana stood on the top of the stairs, pointing the video camera down at them. It illumed a small yellow flashlight beam, the eerie black silhouette of Gertrude.

"Do you see anything? Because I've pretty much had enough," Dana said.

No response.

Gertrude reentered the kitchen, put the flashlight on the kitchen table and went outside. Barney led the way. Everyone else followed. After inspecting the garage briefly, she walked to her Intrepid.

They stopped at the car as Gertrude opened the driver door.

"Do you have any more rules?" Dana asked, pointing the camera.

Gertrude closed the door without saying a word, turned her head, and sneered for the camera.

Ben opened the passenger door. "Thanks for accommodating us. We'll leave you alone now." He got in and closed the door. The passenger window was open.

"No problem," Jackson answered. "We just want to live."

Chapter Seventeen

"Live it up," Bruce Hammerstein said as he passed Gord Sebastian the tubular glass crack cocaine pipe later that evening.

Gord put the lighter to it, sucking slowly as the small yellow flame ignited the chemical concoction. He inhaled, held the smoke in for a few seconds, and finally exhaled a thin cloud of blue smoke that slowly lofted to the ceiling of Bruce's ramshackle trailer. He passed the pipe to Bruce and grabbed his beer off a cheap, scratch-marked coffee table littered with empties.

"I will live it up as soon as I accomplish some goals," Gord said as a brain-numbing sensation of wellness settled through his mind and body. Everything felt all right. But not quite.

Bruce reloaded the pipe and proceeded with a toke. He finally exhaled. With dilated pupils, he watched the smoke slowly drift up, adding depth and color to the newly formed clouds overhead. He set the pipe down, grabbed a beer and took a long pull. "What goals you have in mind, boss?"

Gord had a lot of goals in mind. Aaralyn was none-to-pleased earlier in the evening when he had delivered Emily to Sassy Styles almost an hour late. She had already closed the shop and was sitting in the parking lot in her yellow Volkswagon beetle, waiting impatiently. By the time he arrived, she was really pissed.

"I told you to bring her back at six," she had said angrily after Emily had climbed in beside her. "First you cost me a free haircut, then you make me wait an hour? You think I don't got better things to do with my time than wait for you?"

Gord had felt his face flush from the tongue-lashing, was just about to give her a piece of his mind. Actually, he had a different plan. He was going to grab her bleach-blonde hair, pull her head halfway out the window, and slowly throttle her until she apologized. But a small voice of reason had prevailed and he bit his tongue. He knew she was just waiting for an excuse to sever his joint child custody. He didn't want to give her any more ammo for a court case. He was in enough trouble with the law as it was.

So he had apologized. He said it would never happen again, and left.

Although most of the weekend with Emily had been spent absent of quality time—he played video games while she texted her friends and played on the computer—this story, at least in Gord's mind wasn't all about Emily. It was about winning. It was about control. And he'd be damned if he was prepared to relinquish either.

So one of his goals came down to watching Aaralyn. He had heard through the gossip grapevine she was now seeing a drug-addicted loser in Brantford. Supposedly he was also a heavy drinker who didn't mind partying around Emily, creating a situation that would send the impressionable young girl a negative message. Not that Gord was much better. On the second night with Emily, he had snuck out to Bruce's trailer for a six or seven beers and more than a couple of cocaine tokes. Emily had even asked Gord on his return to the house if he had "been smoking anything funny?"

To which he shook his head and returned to his video game, Metro 2033.

Sure, he indulged. Probably he was addicted. But at least he tried not to do it in front of his daughter. Not like Steve Henderson, Aaralyn's loser boyfriend. No. Steve would have to be watched, his actions video-recorded and used later.

However, Gord's primary goal was to discourage the witnesses to the death threat charges from testifying. If they were too scared to testify, the charges would likely be dropped. No witnesses, no conviction. That would be a good thing. It would help the custody battle that was sure to come.

But who would do the threatening? He couldn't, that's for sure. There was already too much heat on him. If he showed his face around the property again, he was sure it would result in a 911 call. Hell, the tenants probably had Constable Sealing's cell number on speed-dial.

Maybe the answer was right here in front of him.

Bruce had already been briefed on the tenant outburst. And he didn't have many bargaining chips. If Gord kicked him out, where would he go? The worst part would be no source of income for his drug habit. And Gord knew what it was like for an addict to go a few days without crack cocaine. It took one to know one.

"I'd like you to do me a favor or two."

Bruce's eyebrows arched. Favors for Gord always involved something bad. He had been down that road before, and didn't like it. He was quite content to do his drugs, drink his beer, fix the odd car and forget about his past; a troubled past that involved an estrangement from his two small children, and his ex-wife, mother, father and two brothers. Once a successful mechanic with his own shop, drug-addiction had reduced him to living in a trashy trailer and working for a lunatic. Crack had lowered his position in life to that of scum-sucking bottom feeder—a worm in the ocean. But even they cleaned and recycled the ocean, transforming dead and decomposing material back to life. He couldn't say that for his own selfish existence.

"What do you want?" he asked wearily.

"I want you to pay a visit to our new tenants."

He protested. "I've already been there with Ben. I helped him put up the signs."

"Well, I need you there again—this time to threaten them."

"What do you want me to say? And how do you know they won't rat me out? I don't want to end up in jail." Bruce had done a few years already for auto theft and holding up a convenience store, the inspiration borne of a need for money to buy more drugs.

"Don't worry, they won't find out."

"How do you know?"

"Listen, I'll think of a disguise for you, okay?"

"I don't know."

Gord took another swig of his beer. "Well, I don't know what you would do if I kicked you out?"

"You wouldn't do that." But Bruce knew Gord wouldn't hesitate to turf him if his orders weren't obeyed. He had threatened as much in the not-too-distant past. Among other things, Gord was a control freak.

"You want to try me?" Gord asked.

Chapter Eighteen

"You want to try it?" Dana asked Jackson the following evening.

"No," Jackson said, staring at the Beretta 92A1 nine-millimeter handgun on the kitchen table. "It's a gun."

"I know it's a gun. It might come in handy."

Her daughters were upstairs, playing on their respective computers, out of earshot.

"Where did you get it?"

"Rusty gave it to me—partial advance payment for a job."

Jackson wasn't a fan of guns, even for protection. He thought about Canada's neighbor south of the border. According to some estimates, the United States had nearly three hundred million guns in circulation—almost as many as the entire population—and nearly 12,000 gun homicide a year. And the recent senseless massacre in Aurora, Colorado, where a man had purchased multiple firearms legally off the internet and, fitted with legally-purchased body armor and a gas mask, walked into a theatre, setting off tear gas grenades, killing twelve people and wounding fifty-eight others. A cruel irony—they were watching a midnight screening of a film entitled *The Dark Night Rises,* a batman movie. The killer was disguised as the Joker.

Jackson liked being Canadian, thank you very much. He liked living in a country where gun legislation was much tougher than it was in the United States, gun-related deaths far lower, even per-capita.

But Jackson, a news-junkie, knew that the recent unspeakable violence would probably not prompt politicians to change US gun laws. He had read that some US politicians were claiming it was a political faux pas to favor legislation that went against opinions of the National Rifle Association, a powerful gun lobby group. One politician had even gone so far as to call it "political suicide."

So, the status quo with respect to gun legislation in the US would probably remain. He felt Canadian politicians seemed to understand the ease of availability of guns had a direct correlation and causation with high murder rates, suicides, and gun-related accidents. He also knew that most of the illegal guns that found their way into Canada probably came from south of the border.

So he was shocked when Dana had pulled a black towel away from the kitchen table, revealing a black handgun. He didn't even want it in the house. "I don't think I like this idea too much."

"What do you expect me to do?" Dana asked, brandishing the weapon. "Our lives are in danger."

"Is it loaded?"

"Of course it's loaded. This model has a magazine that holds seventeen nine-millimeter bullets. Do you think that's enough to get us out of trouble?"

"I don't want to think about it." Jackson frowned.

"Well, I'm not going to stand idly by while our lives are in danger. Who knows when we'll be able to get out of here?"

She had taken some steps to that end today, but hadn't gotten very far. She had viewed the property her daughter Hillary had found on the internet, but the landlord had been unwilling to negotiate terms. It probably hadn't helped her cause much when she had accidentally blurted out: "We have to get out of there fast. Our landlords are a bunch of nuts." At that point the small bald man standing in front of her had withdrawn the application he had been about to give her and said: "Thanks again for your interest, and the very best of luck in your future endeavors."

Thanks again? Dana had thought. Had he thanked her earlier? She didn't think so. It was the proverbial acronym, PFO, or please fuck off.

Oh well. At least he had been polite about it.

"I don't want that in the house," Jackson said.

"Are you kidding me? Oh, I didn't tell you I had a little conversation with our neighbor down the road. Guy by the name of Hank. According to Hank, Gord has been in all kinds of trouble with the law: marijuana grow-ops, home invasions, violent assault. He said the only thing Gord understands is a shovel to the back of the head. Hank knocked him out with one. Since then, Gord hasn't bothered him. He also said if he sees Gord on his property again, he's going to shoot him. Do you think Gord doesn't carry a gun?"

"I don't know," Jackson said, the realization slowly sinking in. This was a battle he wasn't going to win.

"And he's got every reason to be extremely pissed off at us right now."

Jackson knew there was no longer any point to arguing. The gun would stay in the house whether he liked it or not. The only question now was, did he want to anger an armed woman with fire in her eyes? He had been so pent up lately he had thought of approaching Gord and tearing a strip out of him. He was about to do just that one day, but at the last minute some voice of reason had prevailed and he changed his mind. He didn't know how it might unfold, but he didn't put it past the Sebastians to charge him with uttering death threats if he opened his mouth to their son. And, unlike Gord, who had been released from police custody a few hours after being arrested (money talks), Jackson knew they would probably keep him in jail overnight before releasing him. And the bail, from what a friend told him, would be around $1,500 minimum. No. He couldn't wage war on Gord. They needed all the money they could get their hands on just to get out of this hellhole. He would have to grit his teeth, suck it up, and try to behave like a rational human being. But it was getting harder and harder to do that.

"Okay. I don't agree with it, but I'm not going to argue with you anymore. Make sure you find a good hiding spot for it so the girls don't get it, or see it."

"I've already thought of that. And don't worry, I won't tell the girls. I'm not that stupid, you know."

"Okay ... but put it away, please."

"Do you really think Ben can control those people, mediate this thing?"

"No, I don't."

"Okay then."

Dana disappeared upstairs and reappeared a little while later. "I think I'm going to have tea for a change," she said with a look of renewed confidence. "Would you like one?"

Jackson felt like having a beer, but settled for a caffeine jolt. He nodded as Dana filled the green kettle with water and set it on the electric stove. Soon it whistled and steamed. She prepared two cups of Red Rose tea and set them down on the kitchen table, where Jackson was now sitting slumped over with his head down, hands covering his face.

"Don't worry, honey. I'll only use it in self-defense."

That's what they all say, he thought, but wanted to change the subject.

"Did you make it to the landlord-tenant board today?"

After the house inspection yesterday, Dana had spent most of the day and a good part of the night documenting the terror she and her family had been living in. She had gone some way to writing a short story. She had churned out 5,000 words, and Jackson had helped edit and correct the material. Describing the landlords and their son, she had used colorful adjectives: *intimidating, aggressive, unpredictable, unusual, obsessive and paranoid*, falling short of calling them psychotic. She knew too much judgment and too little facts would not bode well for her case.

Although probably well outside the landlord-tenant board authority, she had also asked the board to examine the landlords and their competency to act as landlords, claiming that in her opinion they were unfit to do so. The letter went on to say Dana and her family would like to prevent any future tenants from enduring the same terrible and traumatic experiences she and her family had to endure during their tenancy.

"It's all filed," Dana said finally, churning the contents over in her mind. "The landlords will be notified. We have a hearing tentatively scheduled for September 12th."

Dana sipped her tea and Jackson gulped his while they talked.

"What do you think will happen?" Jackson asked.

"I think we'll get our money back. This hardly qualifies as peaceful tenancy, which that woman at the board said a landlord is obligated to grant a tenant."

Jackson thought about it. "Those things are a crap shoot. It could go either way. But you're right. They can't rent a home to someone and then proceed to harass them day in and day out."

"No, they can't—"

The living room bay window abruptly shattered and interrupted Dana's sentence. Barney, sleeping on the couch, barked. The crash was punctuated by a rolling thump, like a bowling ball, only one with jagged edges.

Dana raced up the stairs while Jackson ran into the living room. He found a small boulder that had shattered the window and rolled underneath the coffee table. It had a white piece of paper taped to it. He picked it up.

Scrawled in capital letters in black felt pen, the message read: *TESTIFY AND DIE!!!*

Chapter Nineteen

Testify and die. Well if he thinks that's going to scare me, he's got another think coming. Dana stood outside the bay window the following afternoon, holding a piece of plywood while Jackson used a cordless drill to screw it into the window frame. He was halfway through.

The wind intensified as a blackish blanket of clouds rolled in, slowly obscuring the blue sky. A thunderstorm was on its way. And, judging by the ominous cloud formation overhead, it was going to be a nasty one, not unusual for these parts.

"Hold that corner," Jackson said, pointing to the bottom right piece that wasn't quite fitting into the wooden window frame. Dana stepped over and pushed it in with both hands. It resisted, scraping against the frame for a few seconds before sliding into place.

"That's good," he said, and resumed drilling screws.

Last night, the flying rock had shattered more than just the window. To Dana, the fragments of glass littering the living room floor were like fragments of her mind, splintered into a million pieces—jagged edges that perhaps could never be returned to form. Rational thought was giving way to irrational gut reflex. Like a zebra's response in the wild when it senses the predatory lion is readying for a deadly attack, her biological systems were giving way to the demands of the fight-or-flight response, the often deleterious stress mechanism capable of transforming normal behavior well outside the bounds of reasonable reaction and into a black abyss of violent and uncontrolled rage. The same response that leads people to kill and then have no idea of the heinous act they've committed.

It didn't help matters that she hadn't slept a wink last night after the rock threat.

Hearing the loud crash, she had raced upstairs, retrieved the gun, glanced at the shattered glass menagerie, and sprinted outside and down the driveway, a power-boost of fresh adrenaline fueling her rapid progress. Arriving at the end of the driveway, she saw a dark-colored four-door sedan pulling away in the light of the full moon and twinkling stars.

She had leveled the firearm at the disappearing red taillights. Jackson put an arm on her shoulder, yelling "No, no, don't shoot ... please."

But she had not heard the plea. She was firmly in the adrenaline grip of the powerful survival mechanism. She pressed the trigger. But by then, Jackson had grabbed her arm, pointed it into the sky and the round discharged with a loud cracking sound, echoing in the still night.

It was only then that she had stared at him, slowly beginning to register reality, black dilated pupils gradually returning to normal. "Come on," he said. "Let's go back inside." And he had led her away from the middle of the silent two-lane highway and back into the house to the distant sound of dogs barking in the night.

"I think we're going to get a storm tonight," Jackson said, finishing up and noticing her glazed expression. She had not been the same since last night, hell, probably since last week if he really thought about it. For the first time, he was beginning to register an emotion largely unfamiliar to him with respect to his relationship with Dana. And that emotion was fear.

He felt another emotion as well, felt its tendrils slowly twisting and turning inside his head, beginning to envelop and obliterate rational thought, and replace it with a black cloud of simmering rage. A rage that could boil over at any second and rain down a deadly wave of carnage and destruction. He had taken to grinding his teeth in an attempt to control it, keep it at bay. But somewhere deep inside his soul, he felt he was fighting a losing battle. That the rage would take over, consume him wholly and completely and render him incapable of reasoned response. He rolled his tongue slowly along a tooth, stripped of its enamel from grinding, and frowned, consciously opening his mouth to avoid further damage.

"They're calling for as much as three inches of rain, heavy winds and possible hail," Dana said.

Jackson stared blankly.

Thunder boomed and echoed through the darkening skies like a rolling bowling ball. It started to rain.

"Earth to Jackson," Dana said. "I thought I was the spaced-out one. Let's get inside."

"Sorry," he said. "Daydreaming."

The plywood securely fastened, they picked up tools and leftover pieces of wood and carried them into the garage. By the time they returned to the house, it was pouring buckets, high winds dramatically swaying tree branches forcefully with a steady swooshing sound.

They were soaked. A few minutes later they had changed and sat at the kitchen table, opting once again to drink tea as they listened to thunder, high winds, and sheets of pelting rain batter the house.

Perhaps it was an unspoken understanding, but they were both afraid of what might happen to their faculties if they were impaired by the judgment-disabling effects of excessive alcohol. They were already living precariously balanced on the edge. They didn't need an alcoholic shove to catapult them careening helplessly into a dangerous abyss of no return.

Instead they smoked cigarettes, drank hot tea, and did the only thing they could think of—search for a new home on the internet.

About thirty minutes later, as they were discussing some possibilities, Hillary emerged from her virtual life upstairs. "Mom, can I go see Brad today?"

"I don't think so, honey."

Hillary frowned. "But you told me last week you'd take me."

Dana paused and looked outside. The rain was starting to let up, the gray-black sky turning blue as the storm sought other targets.

Brittany emerged, walked over to the fridge, and extracted a can of Coke, popping the cap and taking a long drink. "Can I go see Shelly today?"

"Jackson needs the truck to deliver the cabinets today ... if the rain lets up."

"What about Jackson's car?"

Jackson glanced away from the computer screen. He wasn't the biological father of these girls, but he did his best to be a good role model. Their father Trent had died in a car accident almost ten years ago. A dead-beat dad, Trent's influences had been few and far between. He wasn't around enough to be a good role model. It didn't help that he was often in trouble with the law—a petty criminal.

Jackson didn't want to make the same mistake. And his mostly positive influence had already garnered a measure of respect from the girls. He knew they would probably never call him Dad, but that didn't bother him. All he had hoped to do was give them some proper direction, lead them down a path to a better future. Something, he felt, in some ways he had failed at. "Go ahead and take my car, Brittany. If you want, you can take Hillary to see Brad."

The girls' eyes brightened as they looked at Dana for approval.

After a short pause, she nodded. She knew the girls were also feeling the stress, and it would do them a world of good to escape this hell-hole for a while. And, besides, she could no longer use the thunderstorm as an excuse. It had dumped a lot of rain, but had disappeared just as quickly as it had rolled in. "Go ahead. But make sure you don't stay out too late. Take your phones and call me if anything happens."

Barney, in the living room, precipitously started barking at the bay window.

Dana jerked her head instinctively and raced into the living room, followed by the others. She peered out the window to see what the commotion was about. Barney rarely barked unless there was a threat, and even then, half the time he was too good-natured to bother.

It was Hillary who spotted it, just as Dana was poised to dart upstairs. "It's a rabbit, look."

Dana froze, took a few deep breaths and slowly felt her thumping heartbeat slow.

A multi-colored jackrabbit had bounced onto the lawn. Now it sat quietly, surveying its surroundings curiously, oblivious to the mayhem that was about to explode.

Hillary opened the front door and the rabbit scurried away. Barney had lost interest and returned to his nap. A few minutes later, Dana heard Jackson's Camry start up and leave.

She wondered as she stared out the window at the disappearing car if she had made the right decision to let the girls go into Brantford. The nauseating knot in her stomach was telling her something else entirely—that it was the worst decision she had ever made in her entire life.

Chapter Twenty

Life throws you curves. You just have to roll with them. Or, so Dana tried to convince herself later that evening sitting on her living room couch while she clutched the Beretta and waited for Jackson and the girls to arrive home. She wasn't doing a very good job. Occasionally, she would nervously glance out the window at the sound of a car passing, wondering if it would pull into the driveway.

Barney slept a few feet away, snoring.

She flicked the television to the weather station to check the time: 7:36 pm. *Should I call the girls? Hell, it's still early. They'll think I'm a worrywart. Better wait a little longer.*

She heard the rumble of an engine and started. Barney lazily raised an eye, shifted, and closed it again.

She ran to the front door and opened it.

It was Jackson. Thank God.

He turned off the ignition, exited, and grabbed a case of Kokanee beer from the truck bed. He approached Dana. "How's it going, honey?"

The firearm was concealed in the crotch of her pants, covered with a t-shirt. "Thank God you're home."

He stepped on the porch and kissed her. "I got us some beer to celebrate." He continued into the house and she followed.

"Celebrate what?"

He set the beer down on the kitchen table, pulled out a wad of cash from his jeans, and waved it around. "I got paid today."

"How much?"

"A thousand bucks. And I've got another thousand coming next week, after the installation is complete."

"Well done." She hugged him.

He reached into the case, pulled out two beers, cracked them open and handed one to Dana. They drank, in spite of earlier misgivings about what alcohol might do to already impaired psyches.

"To getting the hell out of hell," Jackson said and they clinked cans.

"I'll drink to that."

"The girls aren't back yet?" he asked.

"No."

"Well, it's not that late."

But the troubling scenarios swirling in Dana's mind had gotten the better of her. She had already envisioned a number of horrific fates and she couldn't wait any longer to find out if they were okay. "Anyway, I'm going to call Brittany," she said, trying to act calm.

She dialed the number and it went to voice mail. After leaving a message, she dialed Hillary's cell phone; voicemail again, so she left another message.

She stared at Jackson, who had lit a smoke and sat at the kitchen table. Her face was turning white. "They're not answering."

"It's probably nothing. You know how kids are, especially these younger generations." But his words were absent of a convincing tone. "Wait until I have a shower. We'll figure this out." He disappeared up the stairs.

Dana fidgeted nervously for a few minutes, listening to the water running.

She made two more calls. One to Brad's mom, the other to Shelly's mom. She was told the girls had left over an hour ago.

Over an hour ago? It's a forty-minute drive. Where are they?

She couldn't wait any longer. She hastily scrawled a note to Jackson, telling him she would be back in a few minutes. She was going to look for them. Something wasn't right. And the longer she waited, the more panicked she became.

Let Jackson chill for a few minutes on his own. He's worked a long and hard day.

Outside, she fired up the truck and headed down the highway.

Fifteen minutes later, gripping the wheel tighter—wide-eyed and jaw-dropped—she saw it. Against the backdrop of the crimson sun setting on the distant horizon, two small red lights twinkled in the distance. Driving closer she was horrified to see Jackson's car wrapped around a telephone pole, the frontend completely demolished. The car was halfway up the other side of a ditch, and a skid trail marked its trajectory as it had lost control and careened off the road. Steam hissed from the motor and swirling smoke ascended into the night sky.

She rushed to the vehicle and peered in the broken driver's side window. Brittany's head had smashed through the windshield on impact and bounced back. Bloodied and cut, it now rested at an odd angle on the steering wheel. Her eyes swept over to the passenger seat. Hillary's head had also collided with the windshield and snapped back. She was slumped over to one side, shards of broken glass protruding from the head wound. Her right arm was in an awkward position, clearly broken. The windshield had two circular imprints where their heads had impacted.

The girls were unconscious. Or dead.

With a short, shrill scream, she frantically pulled at the driver door. But the frontend was mangled so badly it had crunched the doorframe, making it impossible to open. She hurried around to the other side, but that door was also badly crushed in. After a few tugs, she realized opening it would be impossible.

"Help me ... help me ... help me ... please ... someone!"

But no one came.

A few seconds later, she calmed herself down and peered in the passenger side window. She froze when she saw a steady stream of blood snaking down Hillary's head wound and puddling in her lap.

Then some voice of reason slowly prevailed. *What are you doing? You can't pull them out. What if they're badly injured and you make them worse?*

A spark ignited under the hood with a pop and hiss. Dana could smell gas.

She ran to the truck to retrieve her cell, now more terrified than ever that the vehicle might explode.

She dialed 911. A woman answered with a voice so calm she could have been doing her nails. Dana shouted into the phone: "Help me please ... my daughters ... they're dying!"

Chapter Twenty-One

"I'm dying, Mom," Brittany said, looking up with a swollen and bandaged face from her hospital bed three days later. Her head was wrapped tightly in white gauze. She had two black eyes.

"You're not dying, honey. You have a concussion," Dana said, concern etched in her face. Dana had slept at the hospital for two days, concern and worry prompting an around-the-clock vigil. Today doctors had finally told her to go home and at least retrieve a change of clothes; preferably get some rest as well.

According to doctors, Brittany had suffered a minor concussion. The blood and cuts looked worse than they were. She would probably be okay in a week or so, but doctors wanted to monitor her for a few more days just to be sure. The seatbelt had probably saved her life.

Hillary, stubbornly clinging to life in the intensive care unit, had not fared as well. She had suffered a nasty gash on her forehead requiring thirty-four stitches, a severe concussion, and her right arm was fractured in six places, evidently the result of shielding her face on impact.

To add insult to injury, she had regained consciousness for a few hours the day after the accident but then slipped into a coma. She had been relocated into the intensive care unit, where she was receiving around-the-clock attention from medical personnel.

Jackson had been at the hospital earlier in the day, but had disappeared to work. He wanted to finish his painting contract so they could put an end to their living nightmare.

"But my head hurts," Brittany said, trying to move her arm. It was bruised and sore and reluctantly obeyed her command. She brought it up to her head.

"Don't touch that, Brittany. You've got cuts on your head. You'll make it worse."

Brittany sighed and curled her arm on her stomach.

Constable Sealing had attended to the accident along with paramedics after the 911 call. He had taken some notes, asked some questions, taped off the crime scene and continued investigating long after the two victims had been taken to hospital and Dana had left.

Yesterday, he had also dropped by the hospital to ask questions. According to Brittany's accounting of events, they had been run off the road by another vehicle. Only problem was—and it might have been due to the concussion—she couldn't provide a description of it. And due to Hillary's precarious condition, the constable was not able to speak to her.

"Mom?"

"Yes?"

"I think I'm starting to remember a few things."

"Oh really?"

"Yeah."

"Like what?"

"The car."

"Do you know what kind of car it was?"

"It was a green four-door sedan. It was a Ford Falcon, an older one. I know because dad used to drive one. I'll never forget what that kind of car looks like."

Dana thought. Should she tell Sealing? He hadn't been of much help lately. He had not seemed to take Dana's accusations of harassment that seriously. And one comment in particular had stuck in her mind. The words he had uttered nonchalantly when she had first met him, when four young men—riff-raff—were threatening to beat the shit out of Jackson, possibly even her. *"I'm not your babysitter, you know."*

I guess you're not. I guess I'm my own babysitter.

She let the churning thoughts settle: "Did you see the driver?"

Brittany hesitated, perhaps reading Dana's focused expression. It might have been a dead give-away that she had clenched her fists so tightly the knuckles were turning white.

Dana slowly unclenched her fists and crossed her arms. "Brittany, I'm asking you ... did you see the driver?"

She slowly nodded.

"Tell me!"

"It was Gord."

"Are you sure?"

Her recovering daughter slowly nodded. "There's no mistaking the eyes. They were wild with rage."

Chapter Twenty-Two

The rage started boiling over as soon as she left the hospital. Walking in the parking lot in the sun-lit afternoon, Dana wasn't even aware a passerby, a middle-aged man walking toward her, had to abruptly step aside to avoid a pedestrian collision. He shot her an annoyed glance as she passed. She wasn't seeing the reality of what was, only the reality of what would be. She was going to drive to Gord's house and give him a piece of her mind, before returning to the hospital.

And, if he didn't listen, maybe a piece of a forcefully-driven fist.

Leaving Brantford, she reached over and opened the glove compartment. Shit. The Beretta wasn't there. She had left it at home; she didn't want to be driving around with it, particularly while talking to Constable Sealing. He had given her a searching look during their last conversation, a look that suggested he wasn't sure she was fully in control of her faculties. The last thing she wanted was for him to find out she was driving around with an illegal firearm.

But that was okay. Gord's house was less than a mile from hers. She could easily make a quick stop. Her phone beeped, announcing a text message, and she didn't even hear it, her mind swimming with the cumulative effects of sleep deprivation and rage. She gripped the wheel hard, fidgeted with the car radio, tuned in AC/DC's *Highway to Hell*, accelerated and grinned. She might be going to hell in a hand basket. But, at least she was enjoying the ride. At least that's what she told herself.

Pulling into her rented property about forty minutes later, she turned the stereo down and frowned, noticing a pick-up truck parked in front of the house. The warm breeze and hot sunshine did nothing to diffuse her anger.

She stopped abruptly behind the truck—Gord's truck.

Her eyes swept around as she quickly walked to the house. No one was visible. She was going for the gun.

As she was about to open the front door, she saw it, a white piece of paper taped to the glass of the aluminum screen door. She tore it off and opened the door quickly. She ran into the kitchen, where she opened the cutlery tray drawer and extracted the weapon. She had changed its hiding spot.

She clicked the safety off and studied the paper. *Rules and Regulations.* She started to read the paper but a loud, clanging knock on the screen door startled her. She put it on the table.

Barney, sleeping in the living room, started barking.

She aimed the gun at the door and then saw it—the concerned face of Seth Sebastian looking through the window. She quickly tucked the piece in the crotch of her jeans and opened the door, regarding him wearily.

"What do you want?" she demanded, hoping he hadn't noticed a loaded firearm had been pointed at his head. He had come very close to death.

"I want to talk to you."

"Do you know there's a thing called a phone? If you want to come around here, you have to give us proper notice."

He looked at her, defeated, and turned to walk away. As he stepped off the porch, she opened the door.

"What do you want?"

"Gertrude made me come," he said guiltily. "We were notified by the landlord-tenant board you've filed a complaint ... that there's a hearing scheduled."

"That's right," Dana said. "As soon as we find a place we're gone."

"Can't we work this out?"

Dana stepped onto the porch and grabbed the wooden railing in an attempt to steady a trembling hand. "I think we've gone way beyond working this out. I see you've dropped off some more rules."

"Gertrude's doing."

"You guys want to work things out? That's how you do it, by dropping off a bunch more rules, coming around here unannounced, running my kids off the road and trying to kill my daughters? Do you know they're both in hospital?"

"I don't know anything about that. I can take away some of the stuff," he said, waving to the covered items still littering the lawn beside the garage.

"Fuck the stuff," Dana bristled. "Leave it there. You want to take it, you give me a twenty-four hour notice. Otherwise, fuck right off!"

Seth frowned, shrugged, and turned to leave.

But Dana wasn't quite done. "Why don't you grow some stones, Seth? You're such a fucking wimp. Why don't you stand up to that bitch wife of yours once in a while, instead of letting her walk all over you like a dirty rug?"

He put his head down, returned to the truck, and left without saying another word.

She returned to the kitchen, lit a smoke, and picked up the paper:

Rules and Regulations

Rule 1: No parking under any circumstances behind the house.

Rule 2: Do not use the garage. It is not part of the lease.

Rule 3: Do not store items in the basement.

Rule 4: Do not have friends sleep over in the house or anywhere on the property.

Rule 5: Do not use the pond.

Rule 6: Do not go beyond the No Trespassing signs.

Rule 7: Do not disrespect the landlord.

Rule 8: Do not call the landlord after seven in the evening.

Rule 9: Visiting hours for friends are between nine in the morning and nine at night.

Rule 10: No smoking inside the house.

Rule 11: Make sure all hedges are trimmed and lawn is cut at least once a week in the summer.

Rule 12: Do not make any noise past nine at night.

Rule 13: Landlord reserves the right to terminate this lease at any time for any reason.

Chapter Twenty-Three

If he gives me any reason, so much as looks at me the wrong way, I'm going to put a bullet between his eyes, Dana thought as she pulled into Gord's metal graveyard to the sound of Metallica thumping out *Jump In The Fire* from a ghetto blaster:

She eyed the house and the garage.

No one.

She went to the garage, weaved her way around a few auto wrecks, reached the door and opened it. The rancid smell of grease, oil and sweat assaulted her nostrils. She flicked a light switch and overhead fluorescents buzzed momentarily, illuminating the sloppy workspace. Tools, parts, and garbage were strewn everywhere.

A blue tarp covered a vehicle. She lifted the tarp partially and her eyes widened with recognition when she saw it. A green Falcon, with its left fender scratched and smashed in. She examined it closely, wiping her hand over the damage. She lifted her hand. Faint, but visible, was a thin coat of silver paint on her right index finger—a perfect match for Jackson's Camry.

She exited the garage, blinking under the bright sunlight.

Her gaze swept to the trailer, where the music played. She gripped the Beretta tightly and stealthily approached. The door was open a crack, the surroundings littered with beer cans and debris, like something out of a macabre psycho hillbilly horror movie.

Only this wasn't a movie. This was real.

She pushed the door all the way open and looked in. A row of cardboard boxes was neatly stacked to one side. Someone was moving. The remainder of the interior was a pigpen. Then she saw him. A tall, lanky man, his back to her, hunched over the table, steadying a pipe to take a hit of crack cocaine. A pale blue haze of smoke hung thickly overhead.

She picked up an empty beer can and flung it at him. It clanged off the back of his head, knocking his black baseball cap off and spilling the pipe contents.

He spun around, knocking over a full can of beer. It rolled on the floor, the contents draining out.

She leveled the gun at his head.

He stared, wide-eyed with fear.

"Turn that fucking thing down," she said, pointing to the ghetto blaster sitting on the cluttered kitchen counter. "And don't do anything stupid."

He stood up and with a trembling hand killed the power button. But for the chirping of birds outside, the trailer was quiet.

"What do you want?" Bruce Hammerstein asked.

"Where's Gord?"

"He's not here."

"Where is he?"

"I don't know."

She stepped inside the trailer, kicking a couple of cans. They clanged along the floor. "Don't bullshit me. I have two daughters in the hospital."

"I didn't do it."

"I didn't ask you if you did."

She moved closer, within three feet from his face, and leveled the gun to his nose. A bead of perspiration sprouted on his forehead and rolled down his face.

"I won't ask you again. Where's Gord?"

"He went to see a man about a horse."

"That sounds like bullshit."

"No, I'm serious. He's got a hate on for some cowboy who gave him a wild horse last time he went riding. He told me he went to tune him up."

"Who tried to kill my daughters? Was that you?"

"I told you, I didn't do it."

Dana watched a dime-sized wet stain in his crotch slowly grow to the size of a Frisbee, as he pissed himself.

"Who did?" Her daughter had already told her, but she wanted to be sure. After all, Brittany had suffered a concussion and her head wasn't all there. "Don't lie to me."

"Gord did. He tried to get me to do it, but I wouldn't. He's kicking me out." He pointed to the stacked cardboard boxes. "I don't want to go back to jail."

"Who threw that rock through the window?"

Bruce's eyes darted away from Dana—a tell.

"You did, didn't you?"

"Don't shoot me, please!"

"Tell me the truth and I won't shoot you."

"You promise?"

"What ... do you think we're friends or something?"

What little color there was in Bruce's jaundiced face was rapidly draining.

After a moment's pause, he said, "Okay, it was me. But he wanted much worse. It was all I could bring myself to do."

"What did he want?"

"He wanted me to personally threaten you and your friends."

"And all you could manage was throwing a lousy rock through the bay window?"

Bruce nodded, looking embarrassingly at his wet crotch.

"Grow some fucking stones. You want to threaten me, you talk to me anytime and we'll see how far it gets you. You got that?"

Chapter Twenty-Four

"Did you get that?" Jackson's cell phone crackled.

"No, I didn't," Dana said. It was about two hours later, and she was sitting on the living room couch. "I can't hear you."

He was at work, finishing up an interior paint job on a rural property about 14 miles away. The cell reception was bad. "Hang on, let me go outside."

A few seconds later: "Can you hear me now?"

"It's better, but still a little crackly."

"I said I'm going to work late and finish this job. I'll be home late."

Dana took a pull on her beer and a drag on her smoke. "What time?"

"It'll be after midnight. Are you okay?"

With a jittery hand, she lifted the beer. "Yeah, I'm holding up okay. Considering ..."

"Listen, I want to get this job done fast so I can get paid. We have to get out of there or someone's going to get killed."

"I know."

"When I finish, we'll have enough money for another place."

"Good."

"How're the girls?"

Dana had phoned the hospital earlier and was told Brittany was sleeping peacefully and Hillary's condition had stabilized. She was no longer clinging to life. She was of two minds. On one hand, she wanted to return to the hospital and spend the night with her daughters. And on the other hand, a seething rage was fuelling a strong desire for revenge. Fight or flight. In the end, the need for revenge had won. She would return to the hospital first thing tomorrow morning after tracking down and dealing with Gord.

"Brittany is okay. Hillary's still in a coma, but her vitals have stabilized."

"That's great news. I've got to go," Jackson said. "I love you."

"Me too." She clicked the phone dead.

Chapter Twenty-Five

Fuck with me, you'll end up dead, Gord thought as he parked his pick-up truck on the shoulder of the highway four hours later and scrambled into the bushes. Cutting across agricultural fields owned by his family, he slowly and gingerly made his way to the rental property.

The black curtain of night was snatching away what remained of the day.

He had arrived home an hour after Dana had put the fear of God into Bruce. Watching Bruce pack, he could tell by his jittery demeanor that something was wrong. Bruce had initially been unwilling to talk, but two powerful punches to the bridge of his nose had fixed that. Along with the blood spilling out of a disjointed nose, Bruce had also spilled his guts and told Gord everything.

That was the fourth fist he had delivered that day, and he was just getting warmed up. The cowboy who had jury-rigged the stirrups and given him the wild horse had paid for it with two hard shots to the head. But Gord didn't anticipate the man's strength. He was about to give him a pounding, when the cowboy had reared up and kicked him hard in the groin. He had doubled over, wincing in pain, shouting obscenities and rolling around. By the time he had recovered, there were two cowboys standing over him—one with a double-barrel shotgun pointed at his head.

"Get the fuck out of here or get a face full of buckshot," one of the cowboys had said. After very little contemplation, Gord had decided the "get the fuck out of here" option was the much wiser bet. So, like his last trip, he had put his tail between his legs, and limped back to his vehicle like a beaten dog, vowing that somehow, somewhere, someone would pay for this indiscretion.

And Bruce, in the wrong place at the wrong time, had been the unlucky recipient of Gord's idea to pay it forward. But there was still more paying it forward left to do.

He reached a small barbwire fence, extracted his flashlight, and slowly climbed over it, nursing his aching nuts. One more field—one more fence—and he would arrive at the rental.

A few minutes later, he reached the second fence to the sound of a barking dog. Shit. It was the tenant's dog. He gritted his teeth and quickly hopped over it. Barney stopped about twenty feet in front of him. "Here boy."

Barney stopped barking, wagged his tail, and bounded over to Gord. As the dog neared, Gord extracted a small baseball bat, cocked it and delivered a hard blow to the dog's head. Thwack! There was a squeal and a whimper, and Barney dropped to the ground like a ragdoll.

This is too easy. Stupid fucking mutt.

He arrived at the front porch, quietly opened the door with his extra key and pointed the gun around in the darkness, seeing nothing. He knew the girls were in the hospital, the dog now out of commission. He wanted Jackson and Dana, and hoped they were both home. Shining a flashlight, he perused the main floor briefly. He saw the kitchen table littered with beer cans, an ashtray overflowing with cigarette butts. *Good, they passed out drunk.*

He slowly crept up the stairs. When he reached the landing, he searched the two spare bedrooms.

Empty.

He turned the door handle of the master bedroom. It creaked slightly as it slid open and he shone the light at the bed. Dana, in white lace bra and white panties, lay stretched out on her back, by all appearances dead to the world. Or, at least she would be soon enough.

He approached the side of the bed and stared down at her face, calm and serene in sleep as it would be in death. Through the venetian blinds, the moonlight painted gray lines across her body. The blankets had slipped down to her knees.

He pulled out the Glock and pointed it at her head. He was about to pull the trigger, but stopped abruptly. *This is no fun. I want to see her suffer.*

He extracted the baseball bat. Then, on an impulse, tore her bra off in a quick jerking motion, smiling at the perfectly-proportioned breasts that spilled out and greeted him.

Her eyes slowly opened as she swam up from sleep. Then her jaw dropped as the terrifying reality sunk in.

He cracked her over the head hard with the bat—thwack!

Dana saw stars as her head jerked to one side. She heard the words: "You want to fuck with me, you little bitch? Well, here's what you get when you fuck with me."

Thwack, thwack—he cracked her over the head two more times.

Her vision blurred as she felt the warm blood squirt from a head gash and snake down her face, into her eyes. She felt the world turning black. With a sudden strength borne of the need to survive, she struggled to control her darkening world and rolled off the bed, grabbing a bedside lamp as she hit the floor with a thud.

Gord hurried around the bed and was on her instantly, swinging the bat quickly. She held the lamp up and the bat connected with a popping sound, shattering the small bulb and knocking the lampshade across the room.

As another swing came down, she rolled—and at the same time—jabbed the broken glass edge of the lampshade into his crotch. It tore through jeans and a red spot appeared.

"You fucking little bitch," he shouted, doubling over, but only for a second. He dropped the bat, extracted the Glock, and took aim.

Dana frantically grabbed a pillow and threw it at him. A bullet ripped through it, tore into the wall, and a swirl of feathers danced in the air, slowly settling to the ground.

He shot again, a deafening crack. She felt a bullet rip into her left shoulder, blood spurting out and forming a little red river across her bosom, down her belly.

She rolled again and another bullet crunched into the hardwood floor.

He stepped forward, kicked her in the head, and leveled the gun.

It's my time, Dana thought as darkness enveloped her senses. *It's my time to die.*

Click, click. Gord glared at the gun, eyes narrowing. It jammed. "Fucking piece of shit."

He tossed it away angrily, grabbed the bat and attacked. With foggy resolve, she slid her good arm under the mattress, grabbed the Beretta and pointed at his charging head.

"You fuck with me or my family and you die. THAT'S RULE 14!!"

She squeezed the trigger twice—crack, crack—and two bullets penetrated his head, one right between the eyes. His eyes opened wide. He twitched fitfully and, carried forward by inertia, took two steps and fell dead, landing on her with a thud, knocking the wind out of her. His head collided with hers with a hard smacking sound.

Her world darkened. She lay bleeding to death.

As blackness closed in, one thought swirled in her mind: *In death, maybe I'll find peace.*

Chapter Twenty-Six

When am I going to have some peace? Seth asked himself, aggressively swirling a paintbrush with black paint over a white canvas in his studio.

He didn't know it yet, but five minutes ago his son had been shot to death, and his tenant was now bleeding to death. Not that he would have missed Gord all that much, anyway.

He had heard Gertrude the first time, but ignored her. He knew it wouldn't be long before she shouted again.

"I told you, get your ass in here for dinner," she yelled from the house. "And whatever you do, don't leave your baseball cap behind again."

He said nothing, only continued painting the squiggly lines. A few seconds later, he set the brush down and stared at the symmetry of the black lines, wondering what they resembled. Then it came to him—a distorted prison.

"Seth, do you hear me?"

"I'm coming." He moved to a small closet, grabbed a duffle bag, switched the lights off and went into the house.

"Put your hat on the hook," Gertrude said as he entered and kicked his black boots off. He set the duffle bag in the closet and slid the door shut. He removed the cap and carefully placed it on the hook, then walked into the kitchen while Gertrude set the table.

He turned the kitchen tap on.

"How many times do I have to tell you, go wash your hands in the bathroom. This kitchen is for cooking."

He hung his head, went into the bathroom, and washed his hands. *Another kick in the ass.*

When he reappeared, Gertrude was pulling baked potatoes from the oven. He went to the closet, retrieved the duffle bag, sat at the kitchen table, and set it down on the floor beside him.

Gertrude put the potatoes on a plate and set them on the kitchen table. Seth reached for a potato, peeled the tinfoil, cut it with a knife, and began spreading the butter.

Gertrude did the same. "It was a bloody long day today. I talked to that Constable Sealing for almost an hour. He said something about searching Gord's property; that he's going to get a search warrant and return. I'm sure our boy wouldn't be involved in anything like that terrible accident. Do you think he could do something like that?"

Seth shook his head, grimacing as he cut into the steak. *Well done. Again.*

"Have you heard from Gord today?"

"No." He bit into a piece of leather.

"I thought he was coming over for dinner?"

"I thought so too."

There was a moment's pause as they chewed their food.

"You get the rules to the tenants okay?"

He nodded.

"Any problems?"

"Not really."

"Not really? What the hell does that mean? Either there were problems or there weren't."

He unzipped a flap from the green duffle back, extracted a 12-gauge double-barrel shotgun and leveled it at her head. "I guess there were some problems."

Gertrude stood up instantly, her eyes widening in shock. "No!"

"Yes," he said calmly. He pulled the trigger and blew her brains out, splattering brain matter, blood, skull and skin on the kitchen counter top, sink and backsplash. She careened back, striking the counter top, and slowly withered to the floor. Her body twitched for a few seconds before she died.

Seth pushed his plate aside and grabbed Gertrude's plate. He knew she ate her steak rare, just how he liked it. He cut off a tender slice, dangled it in the air for a second, and bit into it, chewing loudly and grinning. *I'm starving.*

Epilogue

"I'm starving," Jackson said, leaning over Dana at the barbeque. He hugged her from behind.

"Careful," she said. "It's still a little tender there." She was referring to her gunshot injury at the hands of the late Gord Sebastian. Luckily, the bullet had not penetrated any major organs.

"Sorry, baby."

"No problem. How do you want your steak? You're usually medium-rare, right?"

"Yeah, but this time I think I'll have it rare."

"Okay. Go check the potatoes. They should be ready."

Jackson disappeared through the sliding-glass door of the split-level townhouse while Dana continued barbequing the steaks.

She flipped them, sat down on the wooden picnic table on the little tuft of lawn that was their backyard and glanced around. It was barely past one in the afternoon on a hot, humid Saturday, but already the neighbors were gearing up for another party. AC/DC's *Hell's Bells* thumped out from a stereo inside an apartment two doors down. Occasionally, an empty beer can would fly out the back door and add to the large pile already littering the lawn.

She lit a smoke, took a long drag, and exhaled. She popped open a can of Molson Canadian and took a long pull. *The more things change, the more they stay the same.*

They had come full circle, now living back in the dumpy townhouse complex where they had started off almost a year ago to the day. Not the same unit—but the same run-down, riff-raff infested complex. But at least this time they were happy to be here, grateful to have escaped Rural Route 14 with their lives. She now had a steady clientele of bikers and she had been doing a stellar and creative job airbrushing gas tanks. She had become good friends with Rusty, who told her, "If anyone bothers you in the future, don't take the law into your own hands, you come to me."

Jackson was also busy with his painting and carpentry work. They might be living in a dump, but at least they could see a light at the end of the tunnel. Their respective businesses were thriving, and they were saving up to buy a house, finally starting to get ahead—in their forties. Oh well, better late than never.

She felt something like sandpaper on her finger and looked down. Barney, licking her hand, looked up curiously. She stroked him affectionately. As it turned out, perhaps he was like a cat and had used up one of his nine lives. The blow to the head had knocked him unconscious but otherwise he seemed none the worse for wear. Even a vet examination had revealed no serious or permanent injuries.

Divine intervention?

Dana didn't know, but she was elated to be alive. And grateful that Brittany's concussion had proven to be a mild one. She had made a full recovery. Other than a few scars on her forehead, a permanent reminder of that terrible day, she was the same old Brittany, surfing the internet, posting on Facebook, but now a little quicker to smile. Perhaps the ordeal had given her a better appreciation for life.

She knew for certain it had for Hillary. Her coma had lasted six weeks, and just when doctors were discussing the possibility of pulling the plug, she had miraculously regained consciousness. And her quirky sense of humor had returned with a vengeance, although at times she struggled with short-term memory loss. Doctors said only time would tell if she would ever make a full recovery.

Dana had suffered some memory loss after the near-death struggle that inspired Rule 14 and Gord's death. But her doctor had said brain scans showed no damage, although at times she gapped out. Again, time would tell if her mind would fully recover. She knew the physical and mental scars were still healing.

But, at least they were healing on the outside of prison bars instead of on the inside, like Seth Sebastian, who was serving ten years for the murder of Gertrude. It seemed like he had finally grown some stones.

Dana had been lucky to get a six-month probation term—which she had served out—for possession of an illegal firearm. Gord's death was ruled a case of self-defense. Constable Sealing had said, "If you tell us where you got the weapon, I can try to get the weapons charge dropped altogether."

Of course, she didn't believe him. And, even if she did, she would never rat out The Skeletons or Rusty. There was way too much on the line. So she had stuck to her story, although no one believed it, that she had found the gun in the wastebasket of a Safeway supermarket parking lot in Brantford.

She stood up and went to the barbeque as Jackson reappeared. "The potatoes are done. How are the steaks?"

"They're done. Call the girls."

"Okay. We have a guest."

"What?"

A tall, lanky man stepped out onto the patch of lawn, his face less gaunt, his complexion less jaundiced than when Dana had first met him.

"Mmmm ... smells good," Bruce Hammerstein said, rubbing a hand over a clean-shaven face, brushing it through a mop of wild hair, and setting a case of beer on the picnic table.

"Bruce, how you doing?" Dana said, giving him a hug.

He smiled a toothy grin. During their exodus, Bruce had befriended Dana and Jackson, apologized for his role in their misery, and they had become friends. Bruce never told the police she had threatened him with a gun.

Dana, for her part, never told Constable Sealing that Bruce had tossed the rock through the family's window. No one was perfect, after all, and Bruce had taken great pains to become a better person. While he had not been able to kick his occasional alcoholic binge or cigarette habit, he was free of crack cocaine—hadn't touched it in over six months. He had moved into the same complex as Jackson and Dana, and was renting a room from a neighbor. Jackson had taken him under his wing and hired him as a painter. He was now gainfully employed and a hard worker to boot. A man trying to better the shitty hand he had been dealt in life.

The girls appeared and sat down for dinner.

After some small talk, Jackson looked at Dana, grinning.

"What're you hiding?" she said.

He pulled out an envelope and opened it, waving a check around and chuckling; his signature laugh, booming louder than ever. Barney barked.

"What's that?" Dana said, smiling. "I can't take the suspense."

"It's a check from Seth for ten thousand dollars, along with a card, apologizing for what they put us through."

He handed the card over. Against a red backdrop was a picture of a big brown teddy bear sitting on a white pillow, one of his paws held to an eye. The bear was wiping away a tear. In large white capital letters, the heading said: *I'M SORRY!*

She opened the card:

> *I'm so sorry for causing you and your family so much grief. I know this check will not replace the suffering you endured at our hands, but I hope it will go some way to compensating you. Please accept my deepest apologies and please forgive me. Although I am now in jail, I am in a much better place mentally than ever before.*
>
> *You were right, Dana. I finally grew some stones.*
>
> *Fondest regards, Seth.*

She couldn't help brushing away a tear as she closed the card. The family and guests stared at her, unwilling to start dinner until she gave the go-ahead.

Finally, Dana said, "Let's drink to Seth Sebastian. Here's to a man who finally grew some stones." *Maybe things are finally starting to change—for the better.*

Hillary and Brittany giggled. They clinked glasses and cans, to the distant tune of *Highway to Hell.*

"Let's eat," Dana said.

"My steak is perfect," Jackson said, holding up a blood-red morsel.

"I hope mine is," Dana said. "I'm starving."

Also by William Blackwell

Phantom Rage, Poison Rage, Infected Rage
Nightmare's Edge
Resurrection Point
A Head for an Eye
Rule 14
Assaulted Souls
Assaulted Souls II
Assaulted Souls III
Blood Curse
Black Dawn
The Strap
The End is Nigh
Orgon Conclusion
Freaky Franky
The Witch's Tombstone
In Your Dreams
Tales of Damnation
Macabre Alley
Brainstorm
The Dark Menace

In Your Dreams Preview

"On the surface, it's a gripping horror thriller with brutal, shocking twists. But beneath that, it's a thought-provoking exploration of obsession, loneliness, and the terrifying power our subconscious holds over us. The writing is bold, cinematic, and immersive—it reminded me of a cross between Clive

Barker and early Stephen King, yet with a unique, modern edge." -Amazon

"I have finished reading *In Your Dreams*. WOW, just WOW! What an amazing tale. You are one hell of a gifted writer." -Amazon.

"This is an amazing book. Great ending." -Goodreads

Alienated from humanity, Oliver Gimble is a self-indulgent sloth who finds vicarious comfort in binge-watching horror movies and gorging on junk food. During sleep, he escapes into a meticulously constructed dream world where he discovers carnal delight with an enigmatic woman called Stella.

His bizarre lifestyle begins to unravel when he meets Carmen Weathersby, a lonely woman, who in Oliver's mind's eye mysteriously transforms into Stella, the woman of his dreams.

But soon Oliver realizes Stella is actually interfering with his new relationship and will go to any lengths, even murder, to possess him.

When Carmen's elderly mother suffers a heart attack, fingers point to Stella. Suddenly, people close to Carmen start dying—brutally and inexplicably.

Careening helplessly down into a cryptic and otherworldly realm somewhere between reality and perception, Carmen and Oliver struggle to try and solve the macabre mystery before it's too late.

A multi-layered, horrifying journey of self-discovery, *In Your Dreams* examines the powerful and shocking connections between our conscious and subconscious worlds—boldly questioning the very nature of reality.

About the Author

Canadian dark fiction author William Blackwell studied journalism at Calgary's Mount Royal University and English literature at Vancouver's University of British Columbia. He worked as a journalist for many years before pursuing his passion for storytelling. His novels have been characterized as graphic, edgy, and at times terrifying. Currently living on a secluded acreage on Prince Edward Island, Blackwell finds much of his inspiration from Mother Nature, odd people, bizarre nightmares, and traveling around the world.

Author Comments

Thank you for reading this book. I would be eternally grateful if you would post a book review on your favorite book retailer website. A positive review is the highest compliment a writer can receive. Reviews are crucial to the success of any author and they help readers discover new books. You don't have to say much. A few sentences will suffice.

In other news, I have a gift for you. Complete the signup form below with your name and email address and download a FREE copy of *Resurrection Point*, a dark tale about the horrifying consequences of experimenting with death and resurrection. You're only agreeing to be kept up to date on blog posts, new releases, and freebies. I promise I won't spam you and you can unsubscribe at any time.

Thanks again for your support.

http://www.wblackwell.com/free-ebook/